Matt had no logical reason to be attracted to Emilie, but damn it, he was

No, he had no business liking this city woman, and wondering what her skin would feel like if he touched it with his fingers.

He should never have hired such a beautiful woman. He was getting distracted. He was thinking thoughts he shouldn't think. Like how she would taste. How her soft body would feel against his. How he wanted to kiss *every* inch of her.

He was thinking about taking another cold shower.

All that meant it was time he started thinking about getting married again. There were several nice women in the county. Women who knew how to live with a rancher. Who knew that a new tractor was more important than a trip to Hawaii.

So what if he couldn't take his eyes off Emilie. She might be everything he'd ever want in a lover, but she could never be a rancher's wife.

Kristine Rolofson is one busy and amazing lady. The author of over twenty books, all published by Harlequin, she is also a mother of six! Moreover, her family was named Adoptive Family of the Year for Rhode Island.

Inspiration for this story came on a visit to the Nebraska sandhills and a stop for a vanilla malt in the very small town of Tryon, Nebraska. Kristine drank the shake, bought seven research books and a gorgeous pair of cowboy boots in forty-five minutes. Her husband knew it was typical behavior, but her brother-in-law George was amazed. And soon Kristine was busy writing *The Bride Rode West*, another winning Brides on the Run story.

Books by Kristine Rolofson

HARLEQUIN TEMPTATION
507—PLAIN JANE'S MAN
548—JESSIE'S LAWMAN
560—MAKE-BELIEVE HONEYMOON
569—THE COWBOY
617—THE LAST MAN IN MONTANA (Boots & Booties)
621—THE ONLY MAN IN WYOMING (Boots & Booties)
625—THE NEXT MAN IN TEXAS (Boots & Booties)

Don't miss any of our special offers. Write to us at the following address for information on our newest releases.

Harlequin Reader Service
U.S.: 3010 Walden Ave., P.O. Box 1325, Buffalo, NY 14269
Canadian: P.O. Box 609, Fort Erie, Ont. L2A 5X3

Kristine Rolofson
THE BRIDE RODE WEST

Harlequin Books

TORONTO • NEW YORK • LONDON
AMSTERDAM • PARIS • SYDNEY • HAMBURG
STOCKHOLM • ATHENS • TOKYO • MILAN
MADRID • WARSAW • BUDAPEST • AUCKLAND

To my husband, Glen, who handed me a suitcase, my laptop computer and a box of chocolates and said, "Go to a hotel, honey, and don't come home until you finish that book."

ISBN 0-373-25753-8

THE BRIDE RODE WEST

Copyright © 1997 by Kristine Rolofson.

Printed in U.S.A.

1

IT STARTED WITH A KISS. No ordinary kiss, Emilie realized through a haze of disbelief and shock as she stood in the doorway of a little room near the altar. This was a kiss of great passion and longing. The two people were pressed together in an embrace that could have led either to saying goodbye or into a bedroom. Her fiancé, the man she was to marry in less than twenty minutes, lifted his mouth and released his...lover.

Emilie clutched her purse to her chest. She didn't think about wrinkling her silk gown. She didn't feel the pain radiating from her narrow white pumps. She forgot she'd been searching for a bathroom.

But she remembered she was getting married. Or at least she was supposed to be.

"Emilie?"

Her fiancé's face was a mask of fear. She looked at the person—one of their best friends—who stood awkwardly at Ken's side. There was anguish in that expression, too.

She was rooted in the doorway. Somewhere an organ was playing a medley of Gershwin tunes while thirteen hundred guests were in the process of taking their seats in the church.

"Emilie," Ken said again. "This isn't what you think."

"I think it is," she disagreed, turning her gaze to his. "You don't love me, do you?"

"Of course I do. I always have."

Emilie took a step backward. "You should have told me you were in love with someone else."

"Don't go," he pleaded, not bothering to deny the accusation. He reached out his hand to take hers. "Let me explain."

She wanted to throw herself against him. She wanted to bury her head in his chest and let him tell her that he loved her and always would, that their marriage would be a happy one and what she had just witnessed was only a joke or a figment of her imagination, the result of too little sleep and a very early morning. But Emilie ignored his outstretched hand and straightened her shoulders. "You should have been honest with me."

"Political suicide," he said, his tone grim, "has never been a choice."

"My father—"

"Has arranged the largest, most publicized wedding in Chicago's history." Ken's blue eyes had turned to ice. "We can't disappoint him, Emilie. I'm certain we can work this out."

"No," she said, backing farther out of the room. "I don't think we can."

"We must, darling. What will the press make of this? If you run away from your wedding, it will cause a huge scandal. Your father will be furious. The election's only two months away. You can't—"

"I certainly can." Emilie turned around, picked up her skirt and ran out. Ignoring the cries of her bridesmaids and Ken's three sisters, she grabbed the small suitcase that held her honeymoon clothes.

Paula, her best friend, matron of honor and a vision in pale yellow satin, grabbed her shoulders. "Emilie, what on earth is going on?"

She considered telling her, but the words stuck in her throat. She couldn't destroy Ken, not even now. "Something's happened. I'm canceling the wedding."

"What about your father?"

"Oh, heavens. I need to think about that." She needed to think quickly, but all she wanted to do right now was hide in the bathroom.

"Don't move. I'll go find him," Paula said, and walked quickly out of the room.

A few minutes later George Grayson, a tall, elegant man with silver hair and gray eyes, entered the room full of whispering women. Paula followed him and gave Emilie a questioning look as George said, "Ladies, would you give us some privacy, please?"

The charming smile faded when they were alone. "Last minute nerves, Emilie?"

"I saw Ken kissing...someone else just now."

Her father's expression didn't change. "Surely, my dear, you misunderstood."

"No." Emilie debated whether or not to tell her father the whole truth. But would he understand? Or would he destroy Ken's career? "It was very clear where Ken's heart lies."

Grayson showed no sympathy. "No matter. According to the polls, Ken is about to be elected senator. I am going to be a senator's father-in-law and you are going to be a senator's wife."

Emilie took a deep breath. "No, Daddy, I don't think I am."

"You are not going to allow this unpleasantness to ruin the merger between two political dynasties. We've been planning this for years and I won't allow you to spoil it. Behave yourself, Emilie. You're an adult now."

"I've been an adult for a long time. Haven't you noticed?"

"The only thing I've noticed," he snapped, "is an overwrought bride creating an unnecessary scene." He glanced at his watch. "I'll see you in the foyer in ten, no, nine minutes. We'll straighten this out later.

I'll speak to Ken and tell him you're feeling better. And I'll remind him to show more discretion from now on. He should know better, especially now that he has a lead in the polls."

"I don't think this is going to work." She didn't want to be married today, didn't intend to say her vows and not mean them with all of her heart. And how could Ken stand in front of the minister and pledge his undying love? How could she?

"You are my daughter. It will work, the way everything always does." His smile was cold. "Do we understand each other?"

Emilie nodded. She understood that her father wouldn't support her, but that didn't come as a surprise. George Grayson put George Grayson first, and this occasion was no different from any other. "Yes, Father. I understand completely."

"That's my girl," he said, turning to leave the room. She heard him call to the others. "You can go in now. Our bride was just feeling nervous, that's all."

Paula hurried to her side and whispered, "You look terrible. What can I do?"

Emilie kept her voice low and smiled reassuringly over Paula's shoulder to the young women watching them. "Can you get a taxi behind the church without the photographers noticing?"

"It's that bad?"

"Yes. And we need to get my tote bag and purse out of here without letting the others know there's anything wrong."

Paula nodded. "We'll say we're making some last minute repairs in the ladies' room."

"Thanks." She tried to smile at her friend, but didn't quite manage to succeed. "I don't know what I'd do without you."

The tall blonde patted her on the back. "What else is a matron of honor for?"

Within minutes Emilie was tucked in a cab. "I'll let you know where I end up."

"You're not going home?"

"No. I think I'd better disappear for a few days. The press are going to have a field day with this one."

"I'll hold them off as long as I can, but you'd better hurry." Paula thrust a wad of cash through the open window. "This should help for today. What do I tell your father?"

"Nothing." She would call him later and try to explain once again.

"Let me go with you," Paula offered. "You shouldn't take off like this alone. Tell me what happened, Emmy, for heaven's sake."

Emilie shook her head. Paula would tell her husband and, although she knew Fred was a nice enough man, Emilie couldn't be sure he would keep the information out of the press. No, it was better not to risk it at all. "I can't. But I'll be fine, I promise."

The cab, with Emilie lying on the back seat until they were out of sight of the church, left the alley and sped toward the airport. O'Hare would be filled with people on Labor Day weekend, Emilie knew. No one would look twice at a young woman in a long white dress. No one would know that the sleek gown she wore was a wedding dress designed especially for this day or that she would leave a nine-hundred-dollar pearl-edged veil in the back seat of the taxi for the driver's next customer to find. She would grab the first plane out, and she didn't care where she landed.

She wasn't going to be married, she was through with men, and anyplace would be better than here.

IT STARTED WITH THE SHOES. Matt watched his tiny daughter sit silently while the salesmen fitted her with a pair of sturdy boots, but Melissa's lower lip protruded in an unfamiliar pout.

"Your sisters have the same kind of boots," Matt assured her. "They'll keep your feet dry when you're outside."

Melissa didn't look at him.

"Stand up, honey, and let me see if these fit," the saleswoman said, and Melissa slowly hopped down from the chair. The woman poked at the toes of the boots. "Just right, with room to grow," she told Matt.

"Good. We'll take them."

"I don't want t'wear them now," his little daughter said.

"Fine. Put your sneakers back on."

"I hate my sneakers. They're too tight."

Matt tried to smile at the saleswoman, who gave him a sympathetic look as she rang up the boots on the cash register. The grandmotherly woman must wonder what a man was doing shopping alone with his daughters. Or maybe not. Maybe she saw single fathers all the time. Anyway, it didn't matter what the woman thought. He could ignore her sympathy and he'd appreciated her patience. He let go of his youngest daughter Mackenzie's hand long enough to pull his wallet from his jeans pocket and pay for three pairs of new work boots. Meanwhile Martha drifted toward the girls clothing department, but Matt could still see his oldest daughter despite the crowds.

He took the bag of shoes, collected the two girls and headed into another unfamiliar area of the store to buy his girls some decent school clothes. He wished he had taken Stephanie's offer of help, but that would have led to admitting that she was right and he was wrong. And, damn it, he wasn't ready to admit that yet. Somehow he would make this work. He was their father, after all.

And being a father ought to count for something in this world.

"Daddy!" Martha held up something shiny and black and very small. He guessed it was a skirt. Or a handkerchief. "I want to try it on!"

"No way."

Her face fell and she replaced the skirt on a rack filled with identical tiny clothing. Melissa dropped his hand and ran over to join her older sister. Matt wondered if he should have been more tactful, but there was no way his seven-year-old daughter was going to second grade dressed like a Hollywood actress. He searched for a saleswoman, but the girls clothing department was crowded with shoppers. Mackie tugged on his hand.

When he looked down, she yawned. "Daddy, can we go now?"

"Not yet, Mackie. We've got to buy some clothes first."

"Soon?" she begged, looking up at him with brown eyes that matched his own.

"Soon," he promised, and led her to an empty chair beside a nearby mirrored pillar. "You sit here with the shoes and rest while I help Marty with her clothes."

"I want to go home."

"Me, too," Matt said, ruffling her chestnut curls. "Stay put and we'll leave as soon as we can." He strode toward his other daughters and wondered how long this final chore would take. He'd thought buying new shoes was hard, but he had the sinking feeling that little girls clothing was going to be even worse.

"I need a skirt," Martha said. "Everyone wears skirts and I'm the only one—"

"Fine," her father said, eyeing the rack of clothing. "Just not something shiny and...short. Where are the jeans?"

Martha rolled her eyes. "I'm sick of jeans."

He ignored that comment. "What size are you?"

"Eight slim, Auntie Steph said."

"And you, Mel?"

The child shrugged, so Martha answered for her. "She's a six, I think."

"Thank you," Matt said, herding them toward shelves of denim jeans. He stopped, surprised they came in so many different colors. "We'll get three each. You pick the colors."

Martha pointed across the aisle. "Mel and Mackie have to get their jeans over there, in the little girls department."

"They do?"

"Yep," Martha said, turning back to the stacks of jeans. "Auntie Steph told us that."

"Okay," he said, taking Melissa by the hand. "You try on the jeans and we'll go find someone who can help us with all of this."

"Can I try on a sweater, too? It has little hearts on it and—"

Little hearts sounded okay. "Sure. We'll be over there by the mirror with Mackie."

Martha smiled, which was a welcome sight. "It's okay, Daddy. I'll be really fast."

"That would be a big help." He negotiated his way past a round rack of pastel sweatshirts, two pairs of mothers and daughters, and headed toward Mackie. He hurried when he saw she was huddled in the chair while a young dark-haired woman knelt beside her.

"Mackie?"

The little girl took the tissue the woman handed her and blew her nose. "Hi, Daddy. Can we go now?"

"What's the matter? What are you saying to my daughter?" He turned to the stranger, who was on her knees by the chair. She wasn't what he expected. She was slim and elegant, with straight dark hair and pale skin. She looked like one of those women in the perfume commercials on television.

"Your daughter was alone and crying. I thought she might have been lost," the woman said, turning her green-eyed gaze on him, then looking at Melissa, who stood silently beside him and gripped his hand.

"Thanks for your concern," he said, watching as she patted Mackie's hand before she stood up and faced him. She wore a long white dress and plastic sandals.

"My daughter was tired and wanted to wait here while my oldest daughter shopped." He didn't know why he felt like he needed to explain anything to a stranger.

"Are you a princess?" Melissa asked.

The woman had the kind of face that lit up when she smiled, he noticed. "No, I'm not a princess," she replied, smoothing the front of her fancy dress. "Not anymore."

"You're wearing a princess dress."

She made a face. "I guess I am."

Matt's hopes lifted. Maybe this oddly glamorous woman was a salesperson. "If you work here, we could sure use some help."

She hesitated until Mackie took her hand. "What kind of help?"

"I'm buying school clothes. Or trying to. My oldest daughter is trying on jeans and—"

"I hate my boots," Mel announced and pointed to the package underneath the chair. "I wanted pink shoes."

"We live on a ranch," Matt said. Anyone with any

sense would understand that you don't wear pink shoes on a cattle ranch.

"A ranch. Yes." Her gaze swept from his denim jacket to his worn boots. "I guessed that. What kind of clothes do the girls need?"

"Jeans, sweaters, turtlenecks. Practical things, warm waterproof things. It's warm now, but it will soon be winter and I'm not coming back to the city any time soon."

Mackie tugged on the woman's hand to get her attention. "Daddy bought a new tractor."

"What color?"

Matt frowned. What on earth difference did that make? "Look, do you work here or not?"

"Green," Melissa answered. "The tractor's green. Like corn."

The woman's voice was gentle. "But corn is yellow."

"The outside's green," the child answered.

The beautiful woman smiled and Matt felt a little light-headed. They would all have to eat soon or he'd be unconscious under a rack of pink jumpers.

"Yes, of course," the woman said. "Green like corn. How old are you?"

"I'm five. Mackie's almost four, and Martha is seven. How old are you?"

"Twenty-six."

"That's old."

"Yes," she said, flashing that smile again. "I am feeling very old today." She bent down to pick up a purse and several shopping bags that Matt hadn't noticed were leaning against the column. Of course she didn't work here. He should have known.

"Me, too," Matt said, taking the package from under the chair. "Come on, Mackie, let's go find your sister. Say goodbye."

Mackenzie Thomson burst into tears and wrapped her arms around the stranger's knees. "No," she sobbed. "I want pink shoes, too!"

"No one is getting pink shoes," he said, realizing that people were starting to stare at them. He lowered his voice. "Mackie, please, come here to Daddy." The child ignored him and the woman looked at him as if he skinned live animals in his spare time.

"Pink like bubble gum," Melissa said. "Pink like the sky."

"The sky?"

"When the sun goes down," she explained. "What's your name?"

"Em...ma. Emma Gray."

Mel giggled. "Gray like...dirty crayons?"

"Gray like...rain."

Matt shook his head. What on earth were they talking about? Gray was gray and pink was, well, pink. "We have to get going."

The woman bent down and untangled Mackie's arms from around her knees, then scooped the little girl into her arms. She turned to Matt, who had expected something very different. For one thing, he'd expected her to walk away. And he'd expected his heart to remain in his chest.

"I'll help you shop, if you want," the not-a-princess offered. "I don't have anything else to do right now except buy myself a decent pair of shoes." She smiled. "Practical, warm, waterproof shoes."

She was making fun of him. Matt didn't return her smile, and if she hadn't been holding Mackie he would've walked away from her. Raising three girls was serious business.

"Will you take my packages, Mr...um...?"

"Thomson. Matt Thomson. Triple Creek Ranch."

"I'm glad to meet you," she said. Mackenzie rested her head on Emma's shoulder and closed her eyes.

"Lady, I'm glad to meet you, too." He couldn't turn down an offer of help, even from a woman in a fancy dress and a teasing way. He knew he'd been a fool to think he could come to the city with the girls and think he could manage everything alone, but he wasn't foolish enough to deny he'd made a mistake. He lifted the bags as Martha appeared with an armload of clothes.

"I'm ready," she said. "These are the things that fit."

"Show me what you picked out," he said, knowing there was something in that pile he surely wouldn't like.

His oldest daughter sighed dramatically. "You have to let me grow up."

"Yeah? Maybe next year, when you're eight. Emma here is going to help us with this project." He rearranged the packages and took Mackenzie into his arms. By this time the child was too sleepy to protest.

Emma didn't take her gaze from him. "Any rules? Restrictions? Preferences?"

"Rules?" He moved a strand of Mackie's hair from across his lips. "There are shopping rules?"

Emma sighed. "I mean, Mr. Thomson, how much of your money do you want me to spend?"

"You get them outfitted and I'll worry about the cost."

She nodded. "Let me check Mackie's sizes and then we won't have to disturb her." She stepped closer—too close, if you asked Matt Thomson—and checked the label on his daughter's sundress. "Okay, this should be easy enough."

"Easy?"

"Easy." Emma shook hands with Martha and introduced herself as her personal shopping assistant.

She scooped the bundle of clothes from Martha's arms and turned to Matt. "You can go back to the chair, Mr. Thomson. We'll let you know when we need you. Okay, ladies. What are your favorite colors? Martha, why don't you try these on for me so I can help a little?"

Matt managed to fight his way back to the chair which was, thank goodness, empty. He arranged his sleeping daughter in his arms, the packages by his feet, and leaned his head back to rest against the mirrored column. He didn't understand the female sex and never expected to, either, but right at this moment he was sure glad that women liked to shop.

"CAN YOU SIT down in them?"

The oldest girl, a fragile beauty with her dark hair pulled back into a ponytail, sat down on the dressing room bench. "Yep."

"And you're comfortable?"

She hesitated. "Mostly."

Emilie handed her another style of jeans. "Try these. Jeans have to be really comfortable or there's no sense wearing them, right?"

Martha smiled. "I'm glad you're here and not Daddy."

"Daddies need help sometimes." Her father certainly had. No, she wouldn't think about her father. He was no doubt searching Chicago for her, though she'd left him a message on his answering machine before she boarded the plane. *I'm going away for a few days. I love you. I'm sorry.*

But she wasn't sorry. Ken was the one who should be sorry.

No, she wouldn't think about Ken, either. Emilie turned back to the child who was in the process of examining herself in the mirror. Girls were easy. If Melissa cooperated as well as her older sister, they'd be done in twenty minutes.

And then what would she do with the rest of the afternoon? With the rest of the day? With the rest of her life?

"These are better," Martha said, sitting down on the bench.

"Great. Let's go see what other colors they have and find some tops to match."

Emilie gathered up the clothes they were buying and herded the girls out of the fitting room. She would have been drinking champagne now if she had stayed in the church and married Ken. The blushing bride would have stuffed wedding cake into her husband's mouth while the video cameras whirled and flashbulbs exploded around them. She would not have been in the middle of a department store while a seven-year-old debated whether she wanted hearts or flowers on her new sweatshirt.

It was good to keep busy. She wouldn't think

about her almost wedding and her almost husband. She held up a sweatshirt painted with a glitter rainbow. "Melissa? I think this is 'you.'"

The younger girl's face lit up. "For me?"

"Absolutely. It has all the colors of the rainbow." She held it up to her. "It's a little big, but sweatshirts are supposed to be roomy."

"Thank you."

"Thank your father. He's the one paying for all of this." Emilie glanced toward the chair where the handsome rancher looked as tired as the sleeping child he held on his lap. The little girl's head rested on a broad set of shoulders. He was tall, with thick dark hair that needed a trim. He was the outdoors type, of course, the kind of man she had never met before and secretly admired. Dusty boots and well-worn jeans were the giveaway there, especially with his tanned skin that looked as if he'd spent the summer outside. Had the man really known what he was getting into with school clothes? Just like a man to think that shopping was easy, that three girls could be outfitted as easily as buying a tractor. And where was their mother? Maybe she was sick, or they were divorced. Divorced, most likely. Still, the girls hadn't mentioned if their mother would approve of their clothes, which was odd.

She wasn't going to ask. Everyone was entitled to their privacy, especially today.

"I really want one of these," Martha said, pausing beside a rack of hideous vinyl skirts. "But Daddy said no."

Emilie shook her head. She agreed with Daddy on this one. "How about a denim skirt instead? They're always great because you can dress them up or dress them down."

"Really?"

"Really." She led her to a rack of denim skirts and helped her find the correct size. "I think you're done, Martha, except for socks and underwear and we'll get those last." Emilie turned to Melissa. "You're next."

In less than thirty minutes they returned to Matt Thomson and the sleeping Mackie. "Mackenzie," the girls told her, was the child's real name.

"Mr. Thomson?"

He opened his eyes and blinked at her. "I guess I dozed off."

"We're done. Everything is with the saleswoman at the counter. You can pay for it there." Melissa tugged on her hand, and Emma bent down to listen. "And we have a special request—pink ballet slippers to be worn in the house."

Mackenzie opened her eyes. "Slippers? Me, too?"

"I guess I know when I'm outnumbered," the rancher declared. He lifted the little girl to her feet, then stood up beside her and gathered the packages.

"We'll meet you in the shoe department," Emilie said, taking Mackie's warm little hand. She wasn't ready to end the shopping expedition and check into a hotel. Alone in Nebraska wasn't how she'd planned to spend her wedding night.

2

"YOU ARE ALL GORGEOUS." And they were, too, with their dark curls and heart-shaped faces. Emilie watched the three girls whirl around in their dance slippers. The two youngest had insisted on pink, but Martha chose black. To go with her new black leggings, she said. Emilie had tried on a pair of walking shoes while the girls practiced dancing in front of the mirror.

Melissa pirouetted over to Emilie's side and frowned at the sneakers Emilie was trying on. "You sure you want those?"

"Very sure." Emilie wiggled her toes. The plastic sandals she'd bought at the airport gift shop had been a wonderful relief from the pinching satin pumps, but Emilie needed something a lot more practical. She smiled to herself, thinking of the rancher's commands for warmth and practicality.

"They look funny with your dress."

"I have some jeans in my shopping bag. I'll change soon." She'd meant to do it earlier. In fact, she'd been on her way to the ladies' room when she'd seen the little girl crying alone in the chair. She'd bought enough clothing for the weekend. That and what she'd carried in her tote bag would easily carry her through the next few days.

Emilie put the sneakers back in the box and carried them to the cashier. She counted the rest of her money. Between her credit cards and cash, she could live quite nicely until this whole thing blew over. The saleswoman rang up the bill and waited for the machine to accept the credit card.

"I'm sorry," the woman said, giving her an odd look that took in the long gown. It was a look that said *You're wearing a wedding dress and carrying a leather purse, so no wonder your credit card is no good.* "I can't accept this."

"What do you mean?" She wasn't even close to her limit, and an hour ago she'd bought jeans, T-shirts, underwear and socks with that credit card. "There must be some mistake."

The woman ran the card through the machine again, then shook her head. "That account has been canceled. Do you still want the shoes?"

"Yes." Emilie paid for the sneakers and hid her rising panic. How could her father have canceled her cards? He wanted to force her to come home, of course. He wanted her to return to Chicago and marry Ken so the positive publicity would give Ken an edge in the polls.

He wanted to prove to her that she couldn't function on her own.

Emilie gulped. Her father might be right. She'd been gone almost six hours and she barely had enough cash left for a hotel room and dinner. And she'd thought this day couldn't get any worse. She took the bag and turned to the children. "Your father will be here soon, so get your other shoes on and put the slippers in their boxes, okay?"

Melissa did a final twirl, knocking over a stack of shoe boxes. Emilie spent the next few minutes picking up boxes and convincing the girls to sit quietly and put their sneakers back on. They were so excited that they practically pulsated.

"Girls. Behave," a low voice said. The rancher, laden with shopping bags, appeared beside her. The girls stopped fidgeting, but grinned up at him with identical expressions.

"They've been good," Emilie said. "They've been dancing in their new slippers to make sure that they fit."

"I guess that just about does it," he said, eyeing the three boxes that Martha held toward him. "I'm supposed to buy those, am I?"

Emilie fought the urge to argue with him and lost. Suddenly she was very, very tired. "Yes, you are. Every girl should have a pair of dance slippers, if only to pretend."

He shrugged and set the bags in a big pile beside her, then went over to the counter with his daughters following close behind to make certain he actually bought the slippers. Emilie found the large bag that contained her purchases and put her new sneakers inside. She slung her tote bag over her shoulder, picked up her purse and waited to say her goodbyes to the ranch family.

It was time to move on. She wanted to get out of this idiotic dress. She wanted to find the ladies' room and change into clothes that didn't remind her of a wedding and the sight of Ken holding someone else in his arms. She wanted a diet cola and a plate of French fries and a hotel with room service. She could afford all that, at least for one night, if she was careful.

She hoped Matt Thomson would be quick, because she was in danger of weeping and she didn't want any witnesses.

"I really want to thank you," the rancher said, putting his wallet into his jeans pocket and handing the latest bag of purchases to a beaming Melissa.

"You're welcome." She could feel the tears starting to burn behind her eyes, so she glanced toward the girls and said a quick goodbye. "Have a good year in school."

"No!" Mackenzie wrapped her arms around Emilie's knees and buried her face. "No!" the child sobbed.

"Mackie," her father said, touching her shoulder. He looked up at Emilie, who felt her lips tremble as she met his eyes. The man had his own problems, that was certain. "I'm sorry. We've had a pretty tough time of it lately."

Emilie took a deep breath. "I know the feeling."

The rancher attempted to pry his daughter's fingers from around the backs of Emilie's knees. "Sorry," he said. "Mackie, we have to go home now."

"I'm hungry," Melissa added.

"Me, too," the oldest agreed. "Let's go get something good to eat." She came closer to Mackie. "You like hamburgers, don't you? And chocolate shakes?"

Mackie sniffed and turned to see if her big sister was serious. "Shakes?"

"Shakes," her father promised, pulling her away from Emilie with gentle fingers.

The child was not going to be dissuaded so easily. She reattached herself to Emilie's dress and looked up at her. "You come, too?"

Emilie patted her wet cheek. "No, honey, I can't."

"Why?"

"Because, well—"

"I'm sure Emma is very busy," her father said. He gave her what seemed to be a friendly smile. "Unless you're willing to let me pay you back for helping us shop? We're going next door to have a quick dinner before we head home."

She should have said no. She should have unhooked the child's fingers from the satin fabric and rushed to the bathroom. She should have done a lot of things, including minded her own business in Gold's department store. "I should—" she began, then looked down into Mackie's pleading eyes. She was in no condition to resist anyone else's tears. "Sure," she heard herself say. "If you'll give me a few minutes to change out of this dress."

"Yeah," the man said, eyeing her outfit. "That's probably a real good idea. Are you going to a party?" In one smooth move, he managed to remove Mackie from her legs and gather up the packages.

"Yes, but the plans changed." Emilie hung on to the remains of her composure. "Where should I meet you?"

"How about at the restaurant? Grandma's Good Eats, right here on O Street. We'll get a table."

"Grandma's Good Eats?" she repeated with a touch of a smile. "How can anyone resist a name like that? Okay. I'll be there as soon as I get dressed."

Mackie frowned. "No more princess dress?"

"No," Emilie declared, backing up a step. "This princess dress is history."

She made it to the first stall inside the ladies' room

before she burst into tears. Emilie leaned against the wall and wept until her stomach hurt. Once she could get herself under control, she wiped her face on damp paper towels, changed into her new clothes, repaired her makeup and folded her wedding gown into the bag. She didn't know what she was going to do with it, but it seemed a shame to toss such a beautiful gown into the trash bin. The princess dress, as little Mackenzie Thomson called it, didn't deserve such a pathetic ending.

Emilie brushed her hair and surveyed herself in the mirror. Things could be worse, she reminded herself.

She could be with Ken.

MATT LOOKED AT his watch. She wasn't coming after all. He was going to order supper and as soon as they ate, he was piling the children and the packages in the truck and heading home. He couldn't get on Interstate 80 soon enough. He picked up the menu. "I'm going to have the chicken-fried steak. Everyone else know what they want?"

Melissa ignored the question. "Where's Emma?"

"Maybe she changed her mind." Maybe she went to her party after all. Maybe she was relieved to escape from his family after shopping with them for almost an hour. He told himself he wasn't disappointed. And he really wasn't, though it would have been a nice diversion for the girls.

"Is Emma our new baby-sitter?"

"Whatever gave you that idea?" He read over the menu one more time and silently cursed the employment agency who had made promises they couldn't keep.

"Can she come home with us?"

"I'm sure she has other things she has to do." He waved at the waitress and saw Emma push open the glass door and enter the restaurant. She spotted them right away and walked quickly to their booth by the window. The girls' faces lit up when they saw her and Matt slid out of the seat and stood up. She looked a lot better dressed in normal clothes, even if her jeans were so new they looked as if they were ironed.

"She came," Melissa said with awe.

Martha shrugged. "She's hungry."

Matt glanced down at his oldest child. "Good point."

"She likes us," Melissa insisted. "I can tell. She got us slippers."

Matt resisted pointing out that he'd paid for the silly shoes, not the lady in the princess dress. He moved out of the way so Emma could slide in beside Mackie. He waited for her to greet the children and settle her bags at her feet, then he sat down beside her. Matt handed her his plastic-coated menu and wished he'd gotten a table. These booths weren't big enough. "We thought you might have changed your mind."

"Not quite, though I had some second thoughts about barging in on your dinner plans."

"We're glad you came," he said, looking sideways at her. Emma Gray's face was blotchy and the skin around her eyes was puffed up. Being used to female tears, Matt realized that this particular woman had been crying pretty hard and he couldn't help wondering what would make a woman like this one cry hard enough to make her eyes look as if she had hay fever. She was a pretty woman, a high-maintenance woman, he knew. He'd noticed the polished fingernails and the carefully cut auburn hair. And he knew that fancy dress of hers probably cost a couple of hundred dollars.

High maintenance or not, she was having a weepy spell. Probably because she was spending Saturday night eating burgers at Grandma's Good Eats. He hoped she wouldn't cry during supper. He told himself to mind his own business. "You'll feel better after you eat."

She didn't look at him, but a faint blush covered the pale skin over her cheekbones.

Martha shoved the menu closer. "Want a hamburger and fries?"

"That sounds lovely."

Mackie nudged her and whispered, "Don't forget the choc'late shake."

"Thank you for reminding me. That's why I came. For the chocolate shake."

She was good with the children. She knew how to talk to them. She knew how to buy things for them. Was Fate giving him a sign?

"You ready to order, folks?"

Matt looked at Emma again. He liked to think he was a pretty good judge of people. He hadn't made too many mistakes in that department, though he'd made plenty of others. But he knew people, or he liked to think he did. And he was desperate, though he didn't like to remind himself of that fact too often.

"I'll have the hamburger special, please," Emma said and looked at the girls. "Are we all having chocolate shakes?"

There was a chorus of high-pitched yesses.

"Five chocolate shakes and one hamburger special," the waitress said. "And the girls?"

Matt answered. "Three more hamburger specials—kid-size—and a chicken-fried steak. With light gravy and mashed potatoes."

"You got it. You want the shakes now or with dinner?"

"Anytime, thanks." They were all starving. If the

girls didn't eat their dinners, he'd take home the left-overs for later.

The waitress smiled at both of them and collected the menus. "Nice family you have here."

Matt's smile froze. "Thanks."

"I'll be right back with those shakes."

Martha leaned forward and stared at their guest. "Are you crying?"

"Uh, no," Emma replied.

"But you look like—"

"Marty," Matt interjected. "Please don't bother Emma with your questions."

"I just asked—"

"Martha." He put a ton of warning into his voice and his sternest expression on his face. His daughter's eyes widened and she closed her mouth. Matt realized it was up to him to make casual predinner conversation so he turned to the woman whose thigh was very close to his. "So, uh, Emma. Do you live in Lincoln?"

"No." She took a sip from her water glass. "Actually, I haven't decided."

That meant she was either considering taking a job here or she was looking at the university. She'd said she was twenty-six, so maybe she was thinking about going to grad school. "Have you seen the campus yet?"

"No, but I saw the crowds heading for the football stadium. I wonder which team won."

Matt grinned. "You're not from around here then, or you'd know that Nebraska almost always wins."

"Go Big Red!" Melissa cried and a young man in the next booth turned around and gave her a high five.

"I love my slippers," Mackie said, leaning her head against Emma's arm. Matt watched the woman put her arm around his daughter and give her a hug.

"Are you in town looking for a job?" His throat went dry. Could it really be this easy or was he a fool for thinking what he was thinking?

Surprise lit those green eyes of hers. "A job?" she repeated, as if she hadn't heard the word before.

Okay, he was a fool. "You must be a student then."

"No. I mean, I don't know what I'm going to do." She gave him a self-deprecating smile. "I'm at a crossroads, you see."

He didn't see anything but the answer to his prayers.

"We hafta go to the bathroom." Melissa scooted out of the booth, with Martha following close behind.

"Again?"

"Daddy," Martha groaned. "You're not supposed to count."

"Excuse me." He turned back to Emma, the woman at a crossroads who might need a job, but the waitress came with a tray full of drinks and took her time setting them all down in the proper places, delivering straws and napkins and news that their dinner would be here soon.

"Thanks," he managed to say before turning back to Emma Gray. "What kind of crossroads?"

"You really don't want to hear about it," she said, peeling the paper from her straw.

"No, I do. Really." *Tell me you're a nurse. Tell me you're a kindergarten teacher. Tell me you love horses and are tired of cities.*

"I guess you're right," she murmured, plunging the straw into the shake. "I'm going to have to get a job."

Matt took a deep breath. Okay, so she wasn't matronly. "Can you cook?"

"A little."

"Run a house?"

She winced. "All my life."

He didn't hesitate. He couldn't afford to. The girls' aunts wanted to help, but really couldn't. Ruth offered to help, but her arthritis was acting up. Stephanie wanted to keep the girls in Omaha, but he couldn't bear to be separated from them. He'd told both women that he would hire some help. All hell was going to break loose if he didn't even have one job candidate coming out to the ranch for an interview. "Want a job on my ranch?"

"Excuse me?"

"Do you want a job on my ranch?"

Her smile faded. "Doing what?"

"I came to town to buy a tractor and hire help. I need a housekeeper. A nanny, I guess you could call it."

"What about employment agencies?"

He went for the truth. "It's pretty hard to get anyone who wants to live that far out of town. I've had some help, but things didn't work out. The girls spent part of the summer with their aunt in Omaha, but they're home now. It's not easy to run a ranch with a three-year-old on your shoulders."

That green-eyed gaze held his, though she hesitated before speaking. "And Mrs. Thomson?"

"She died. My aunt helped with the girls, but she's got bad arthritis, and running after the girls is too much for her to handle."

"I'm sorry."

He knew she wasn't talking about Aunt Ruth's aches and pains. "Yeah, well..."

The girls hurried back, followed by the waitress carrying a tray piled high with their dinner.

"Never mind," he told Emma. "It was just a crazy idea."

She didn't say anything, but gently nudged

Mackie awake so she could eat her hamburger. Matt kept busy passing ketchup and mustard, rescuing unwanted pickle wedges and making certain that glasses of chocolate shakes didn't get so close to the edge of the table that they fell in someone's lap. He noticed that Emma passed napkins around and listened to the girls' discussion of whether or not they liked tomatoes.

Well, he'd tried. She hadn't said yes and she hadn't said no. He wished he'd had more time to talk her into taking the job. He was desperate enough to think that something this crazy might just work.

MARTHA MADE SURE she took the others to the bathroom when Daddy paid for supper. It was her job as the oldest girl to hold Mackie's hand on the way so she wouldn't get lost. And she was supposed to make sure that Mel and Mackie washed their hands after they were done.

She got to boss everyone around, which was pretty neat sometimes. But now, waiting inside of the stinky bathroom for the others to be done, she wished she was the youngest and somebody had to wait for her. "Come on," she said. "Hurry up!"

"Okay," Mackie hollered. "My panties got mixed-up."

"I'm done," Melissa said, opening the door.

"Wash your hands."

"I know." She marched over to the sink. "You're not the boss of me."

"Yes I am." It was an old game and Martha didn't feel like playing. She didn't have much time. "Mackie, hurry. Fam'ly meeting."

Mel wiped her wet hands on her shirt and looked interested. "Why?"

"Emma needs to come home with us."

"I'm done," Mackie said, opening the door and going over to the sink. She eyed the soap dispenser with glee and proceeded to squirt pink liquid all over her tiny fingers.

"Okay," Melissa said. "Tell Daddy."

"Tell Daddy?" Mackie held up her hands, so Martha turned on the water in the sink and made sure it wasn't hot.

"Rinse," she ordered her little sister. "And hurry up."

"I am," the little slowpoke insisted, playing with the water. "I like Emma."

"She's nice," Melissa observed. "I think she's a princess. She got us pink slippers."

"She didn't make me eat my tomatoes," Martha said. The last baby-sitter had been cranky. Another had made them eat meat loaf. The pretty one liked to talk to Daddy and not read stories. Aunt Ruth was too tired to play and Auntie Steph didn't want them to live at the ranch and was allergic to dogs. Martha didn't want to live with Auntie Steph all the time. What would Daddy do all by himself?

"Tell Daddy," Melissa repeated. "Tell Daddy we want Emma to come home with us."

Martha gave Mackie a paper towel before she got water all over her T-shirt. "Emma might say no."

"No?"

"No?"

"Yeah," Martha said. "She's been crying. I think she's having a bad day."

"Oh." Mackie's lower lip trembled.

"Don't start crying *now*," Martha told her. "Save it for later. All you have to do is hang on to Emma and don't let her go. Like you did in the store, remember?"

She nodded.

Melissa looked worried. "What about Daddy?"

"Don't worry about Daddy," Martha said, making herself sound very brave and very smart so Melissa would be quiet. "I can take care of him."

3

"WHY WOULD YOU offer me a job? You don't know anything about me," Emilie said. She folded her napkin and set it neatly on the table before turning to look at the man seated beside her. Since the three girls had left to use the bathroom, Grandma's Good Eats seemed decibels quieter and she could finally ask the question that had been nagging her throughout the meal.

He didn't seem surprised by the question. "You already passed the first test."

"Which was?"

"Shopping." Matt Thomson smiled a little, making the handsome rancher look years younger.

"I've been thinking about this all through dinner," Emilie began again, "And I—"

"You could *think* during dinner? Another test passed."

"Dinner was fun. Livelier than I'm used to," she said, remembering too many formal dinners with her father's friends. "But still fun."

"You don't have children, then?"

"No."

He looked at her hands, making Emilie glad she'd tucked her engagement ring into the zipper compartment of her purse. "And you're not married."

"No. Heaven forbid. Look, Mr. Thomson, I'm, uh, here on vacation." His eyebrows rose. She supposed Lincoln, Nebraska wasn't exactly a destination resort. "I'm trying to think about my future."

The rancher picked up his coffee mug and took a sip. "Go on."

"Well," Emilie hesitated. What did she want to do? She could call Paula and have her wire money, but she couldn't borrow from her friend indefinitely. She wouldn't be able to wire her bank until Tuesday, since this was a holiday weekend. Or she could call her father and go home. "I'm interested in the job, but I don't know how long I can stay."

"Stay meaning months?"

"Days."

"Days," he repeated, looking disappointed. "That's not going to help me very much."

"You don't even know if I'm what you want. We could have a trial period." What was she doing? Emilie squashed the panic that threatened to make her run to the telephone.

"Go on."

"No, now you tell me what you have in mind." He was the one who brought up the subject of the job.

He should do some of the talking. Emilie lifted her chin and waited, but Matt Thomson slid out of the booth and started picking up packages. He was a man ready to be on his way.

"I need what amounts to a substitute mother," he said bluntly. "You get them off to school, you take Mackie to preschool, you bake the cupcakes and cook the meals and wash the clothes and watch soap operas or 'Melrose Place,' whatever. I don't care as long as the girls are taken care of and are happy." He named a salary, described the medical benefits and told her she'd have Sundays off and the use of the station wagon.

"You'll be one of the family," he added, almost as an afterthought as he shot a worried look in the direction of the bathrooms. "It's not exactly a high-pressure job. And about how long you stay, I guess it doesn't matter. You could take the job for a couple of months, at least until I have time to advertise for someone else and, hell, it beats flipping hamburgers at Dairy King."

It beat dealing with George Grayson's wrath. And how hard a job could it be? Shopping had been easy enough. Child's play, actually. She would be independent. She would have a place to live until she sorted out the rest of her life. Until she could go home. "Two weeks' trial period," she insisted, knowing she'd never be able to stay longer than that.

"I guess you've got yourself a deal. What do you say?"

Emilie retrieved her packages and her bags, then scooted along the bench until she stood beside the rancher.

"Emma!" Melissa cried, her sisters following close behind. "Where are you going?"

Mackie burst into noisy sobs and grabbed Emilie's legs. Martha hung back, though she glared at her father as if daring him to do something to stop the madness. "Mackie, please," Emilie said, noticing that people were starting to stare. "You don't have to cry. Truly you don't."

"Well?" Matt's gaze met hers and she realized he looked exhausted. "Are you coming with us or not?"

"I'm coming," Emilie replied, unable to move with her hands while a little girl gripped the backs of her knees. She set down her shopping bag and her tote bag, then stroked the child's soft hair. "Mackie? You have to let me go."

"No!"

Martha tapped her sister on the shoulder. "Stop it, Mackie. She's coming with us."

"She is?" came the muffled question.

Emilie didn't know what to do. "Yes. If you'll stop crying and help me carry these packages." To her relief, the little girl released her immediately and picked up the tote bag. She beamed up at Emilie as if the previous tears had never happened.

"Okay," Mackie said, shooting a triumphant look at her oldest sister. Emilie wondered if the little girl was mentally disturbed. Was that why Matt Thomson couldn't find help? She grabbed the shopping bag and faced the tall rancher.

"Ready when you are," she said. Mackie's small fingers snaked into her palm and held tightly. "Then we're out of here," the man said, and four females followed him out of the restaurant into the warm summer evening. They turned a corner and were soon walking through a parking lot, but Emilie hesitated when she saw Mr. Thomson stop behind a huge pickup truck. He stored all of the packages under a tarp, unlocked the doors and lifted the girls into the cab of the truck before turning to Emilie.

"You get to sit in the front," he said.

It was her last chance to turn and run, her last opportunity to go home. Emilie straightened her shoulders and walked toward the tall man who held the passenger side door open. Going home was not an option, at least not right away. No, she was going to be a housekeeper. On a remote ranch where she couldn't be found. Emilie climbed into the truck and smiled at the girls in the rear seat. They were sweet children and their father seemed pleasant enough. How hard could the job be?

After all, she wasn't going to be in Nebraska forever.

"Better get comfortable," the rancher said, guiding the truck through town. "We're a long way from home."

"How long?" she felt obliged to ask, though she didn't really care at this point in her day. The farther away the better was what she wanted to say, but she didn't dare. That wouldn't be an especially domestic remark.

"Five hours, maybe more."

"Halfway across Nebraska?"

"Not quite." He smiled a little and stepped on the gas pedal. "But it's going to feel that way."

"I don't mind," she said, turning to look out the window. There wasn't much to see but fields that stretched to the horizon. The sky was going to be dark soon, and this day was going to be over. Emilie leaned back in her seat and hid a sigh of relief.

"I GOT BLACK LEGGINGS just like Jennifer's," the child murmured, snuggling into her pillow.

"Go to sleep now," he told Martha, tucking the pink sheet over her shoulders.

"It's late."

"How late?"

"Late enough," he murmured, turning off the bedside light. Martha's eyes were already closed and, when he turned to Melissa, he saw his middle daughter was asleep with the silly ballet shoes tucked under one arm. He supposed she wanted to wear them in the morning and the thought made him smile to himself. He didn't understand girls, but he'd hired somebody who did. Matt checked on Mackie once again. He'd carried her upstairs and tucked her into bed without waking her up. She wouldn't like waking up in the morning with her clothes on.

Downstairs in the kitchen Emma waited. She looked tired, he realized. She sat at the kitchen table, her bags beside her chair, as if she were waiting for a bus to take her someplace else. She was unfortunately beautiful, she seemed nice enough, and he hoped like hell that she would stay long enough for him to get Stephanie off his back about moving the girls to Omaha.

"I'll show you your room," he said. "Don't worry about the kitchen. You'll have the rest of the weekend to figure out where everything is, and the girls can help you."

He led her to the room that had belonged to his father's sister, Great Aunt Gertrude, and had housed relatives and assorted guests over the many years since Gertie died. Tucked behind the kitchen, it had its own bathroom and a nice view of the east pasture.

"Thank you," was all she said in that polite voice

of hers. He couldn't figure out if she was really being polite or not. He switched the overhead light on and looked around. The furniture had probably been the same for a hundred years, but Matt hoped that was a good thing. Gertie had liked the old things around her and no one had ever bothered to change the room. There were too many other things to do on the ranch than bother with chores that didn't need to be done.

"The bed should be made up," he said. "If not, you should find sheets in the closet over there."

"Thank you," she said once again. "I'm sure I will be very comfortable."

"Yeah, well." Suddenly Matt didn't know what to say. It was late and he was tired and he stood in a bedroom with a beautiful stranger talking about bedsheets. He started backing out of the room. "Don't worry about getting up early to make breakfast," he assured her. "No one will be up before seven."

He left, closing the door behind him, and turned the corner to the kitchen. He turned off the lights and headed for the stairs and bed. After two nights at the Cornhusker Hotel, it was going to be good to be back in his own bed. All in all, it had been a pretty good weekend. He'd hired a housekeeper and bought himself a new John Deere.

GETTING OUT OF the hard bed was almost a relief. Emilie had tossed restlessly there, in the surprisingly cozy room behind the kitchen, until dawn paled the sky and told her the night was over. It was time for coffee. It was time to look around the house and see what she'd gotten herself into. It was time to be Emma Gray, prairie housekeeper.

Because prairie was all she could see from the kitchen windows. Oh, there were plenty of outbuildings over to the left. She was sure there were barns and sheds in that direction. She could see the dirt roads and roofs behind the hills. Sand hills, Mr. Thomson had called them. Welcome to the sand hills, he'd said, when he'd turned off the interstate and headed along a two-lane road. She figured they'd traveled for another hour or so before turning into the ranch.

And she'd had no idea what he was talking about when he'd described his home, but now she looked out the window at the waving pale green grasses and thought of every Western movie she'd ever seen. This is where the buffalo roamed, where the deer and the antelope played.

This is where Emilie Grayson would start her first paying job.

Correction: Emma Gray, Woman of the West, would learn how to be a mother. Not that she intended to attempt marriage again any time soon, she thought, pulling on her jeans. She rummaged through the shopping bag to find a shirt. No, she would probably live alone for a few years until she was at least thirty. She would find a lovely apartment in Chicago, take a year or two to decorate it, and then she would give parties. Emilie put her sneakers on. She wouldn't wait to be married before she bought herself china and crystal and all those beautiful things that were sitting in Chicago and would have to be returned. Her father's latest secretary would be facing a difficult week.

Emilie shook off wedding worries and tiptoed across the hall to the kitchen. She could smell coffee. The kitchen was an enormous room and clearly a place that was used for more than eating. A battered brown couch sat against one wall, while counters and appliances used up two others. A painted bookcase sat in one corner of the room, a rocking chair in another. The counters were almond and matched the appliances; the floor was an odd gray-speckled linoleum that had borne the brunt of many boots.

Mr. Thomson was seated at the oval oak table in the center of the room. His dirty dishes were pushed to one side, his coffee cup was by his elbow. He looked up from the newspaper. "Good morning."

"Hi." She felt shy. "I see you made your own breakfast."

"I usually wait on myself. Work starts early around here."

Uh-oh. "Sorry," Emilie said, heading toward the coffeepot. "I'll have to set my alarm clock."

"I told you not to worry about it this morning." He folded up his newspaper and shoved it to one side. "It's Sunday. My aunt will be over around nine to take the girls to church, so can you get them ready by then?"

"Sure." She glanced at her watch. She had three and a half hours. "No problem."

He reached for his hat. "Good."

"Mr. Thomson—"

He stopped in midstride. "Call me Matt."

"All right. Matt. Could we meet sometime this morning and go over the week's schedule? I'd like to know what the girls do each day."

The man stared down at her. "Schedule?"

"Yes. That would help me understand what I need to do."

"Martha can fill you in. She knows what goes on around here, and Ruth can tell you, too. I have to get back to work."

"Oh. Of course." Clearly her new employer wasn't interested in schedules. This was going to be a do-it-yourself job situation. She watched Matt leave the kitchen, heard a distant door bang shut, and then started opening oak cabinets until she found the one filled with mugs. She selected one decorated with a red football player and filled it to the brim with hot coffee. She took a few careful sips, resolved to find a better brand of coffee beans, and then opened every cupboard, cabinet and drawer in the kitchen to see what was there.

"Snooping around?" a voice asked.

Emilie turned to see a plump gray-haired woman leaning on a cane in the doorway. She wore a faded housedress and there were three plump curlers on the top of her head. She looked harmless enough, even though she wasn't smiling. "Getting my bearings," she corrected, too curious about her visitor to be offended.

"You'd better shut them doors before you bang into one and give yourself a concussion. We don't need any women around here with concussions."

Emilie obediently shut all the doors except for the one that held the mugs. "May I offer you a cup of coffee?"

"I'm not allowed to drink the stuff." The elderly woman shuffled over to the table and sat down in the place opposite where Matt had eaten.

"A cup of tea, then?"

"Nah, pour me some coffee. Doctor Ned doesn't have to know everything."

Emilie did as she was told. "Do you take anything in it?"

"No. Just bring it over here before it cools off. I like it hot and black."

Emilie refilled her own cup and brought both mugs over to the table. "So do I." She sat down near her visitor, but cautiously left one empty chair between them. "I'm Emma Gray," she said. "And you are...?"

"Ruth Tuttle. Aunt Ruth to everyone on the Triple Creek and to everyone in the county, too, I guess. You can call me that, too, so as not to upset things." She took a sip of her coffee and shifted her weight in the chair as if she were in pain. "Darned arthritis."

"You used to take care of the girls, I understand."

"I still do, mark my words, young lady. Matthew told me this morning that he'd hired himself a housekeeper in Lincoln and I had to come see for myself. I'm not much for this housekeeper business, but Matthew doesn't have much of a choice right now with Stephanie breathin' down his neck and giving him a hard time."

"Who's Stephanie?"

"His sister. You'll meet her soon enough. She'll be down here faster than one of them fancy space rockets once she hears about you." Ruth looked past her shoulder toward the stove. "What are you making for breakfast?"

"Nothing yet. Matt said not to worry about it."

The woman's expression showed what she

thought about that. "I suppose he made his own eggs this morning."

"Well, yes, but—"

"That won't hurt him none. Make him take his dirty dishes to the sink next time. You don't want a man getting bad habits and a man who lives alone gets full of bad habits in no time at all, you know."

"Okay." Emilie tried not to smile. 'Aunt Ruth' was serious and obviously considered herself an expert. "Anything else? Matt said you'd be able to tell me the girls' schedules."

"The girls'll need a decent breakfast." The woman's blue eyes narrowed as she took another sip of the forbidden coffee. "Every morning. And none of that sugared cereal stuff, either, though I know they sneak it when they can. It's bad for their teeth. Do you have children?"

"No."

"I suppose not, or you wouldn't be here by yourself, unless you were one of those women who leaves her family to 'find herself.' I don't hold with that."

"Well, I—"

"Are you divorced? One of those man-hating feminists who wants to be called Miz?"

"I'm not divorced," Emilie said, carefully not responding to the other question. "And I've never been married."

"Ever come close?"

"Very close."

"I've had three husbands, one of them was Matthew's great-uncle. My nephews work here on the ranch. You're a pretty enough thing, though you're too skinny, so the men will be buzzing around. Don't pay 'em any attention and don't lift your skirts for any of 'em, either." She winked. "Don't want to set a bad example for the little girls."

"You have nothing to worry about. And I don't have any skirts."

"Hmm." Those blue eyes studied her face. "You go to church?"

She met the gaze. "I was there yesterday."

"We've got a Methodist church in town, decent pastor this year, too. Speaks loud enough so I can hear. The service starts at ten and I like to get there early. Have the girls ready by nine, 'cuz I drive slow." She struggled to her feet and grabbed the cane. "Damn hip," she muttered. "You're welcome to join us. We get back around noon. Did my nephew give you Sundays off?"

"Yes."

Ruth nodded. "Then I'll defrost a meat loaf."

"Don't go to the trouble. I'll make dinner," she heard herself say. "Don't worry about a thing."

"Hmm," was the woman's only response. "You don't look like the domestic type, Emma Gray. Those fingernails of yours cost money."

"That doesn't mean I can't cook," Emilie bluffed. It didn't mean she *could* cook, either, but she'd seen plenty of cookbooks in the cupboard next to the stove. And Paula had told her once, if you can read, you can cook.

"You don't look like anyone's housekeeper."

"I took care of my father for years," Emilie declared, knowing she spoke the truth and yet knowing what she said would be completely misinterpreted.

Ruth Tuttle's gray eyebrows rose in disbelief.

Emilie continued, wondering if the gods would strike her dead for such blatant exaggerations. "Since I was seventeen, I ran the household." Meaning she was in charge of several servants, the selection of the week's menus, and responsible for coordinating her father's social calendar with his business schedule. She didn't know why she wanted to impress Matt Thomson's aunt, but she wanted the woman to have some confidence in who was taking care of the children. There was something about the blunt old woman that Emilie liked.

"Be that as it may, have the girls ready by nine. And don't let Martha Ann tell you it's okay to wear jeans, either. They know what their church clothes are and I expect them to look decent."

"They will." She took Ruth's cup before the old woman could attempt to take it to the sink. The poor old thing had enough trouble with that cane without trying to carry dishes.

"Good coffee," Ruth said, limping out the door. "Matthew must have made it."

"IT'S OKAY to wear jeans," Martha declared. "Lots of kids go to church wearing jeans."

Emilie lifted a flowered sundress over Mackie's head and helped the child find the holes for her arms. "I've never heard of such a thing."

"I don't know if I should wear the black jeans or the purple ones." She held them up. "Whaddya think?"

"I think you should find a dress and put it on." She turned Mackie around and buttoned up the back of the dress. She looked at her watch. "And do it fast, because you don't want to be late for church."

Martha dropped the jeans on the floor and bounced off in a huff. "I hate those stupid dresses! I want to wear my new stuff!"

Mackie handed Emilie a brush and she used it to get the tangles out of the child's long hair. "Put on a dress, Martha. Your aunt expects you to look nice for church. Do you want me to help you pick out something?"

Melissa, fully dressed, crawled back in bed and pulled the sheet up to her chin. The seven-year-old yanked open her closet door and disappeared inside.

Emilie heard the rattle of plastic hangers and the muttering of a frustrated child. She hid a smile. She'd lived in boarding schools for years, so tantrums over clothes were nothing new. "Want help, Martha?"

Silence. Then, "Can I wear my new skirt?"

"No. I don't think your aunt wants you to wear a denim skirt to church, either." Emilie pulled Mackie's hair into a ponytail and decorated it with a pink scrunchie. "There," she told her. "You're done."

"Thank you, Emma." Mackie gave her a hug and went over to the bed to poke at Melissa's arm. "Wake up! Wake up!"

Emilie waited for Martha to back out of the closet. She hoped the child would be cooperative this morning, but the girls were all tired from their trip to Lincoln. Shopping bags and new clothes littered the wood floor in the bedroom that Martha and Melissa shared. Mackie, a light sleeper and an early riser, had her own room only because her sisters didn't want to awaken at dawn. The girls had explained a number of things:

Daddy had a great big ranch with lots of horses and cows.

Auntie Ruth never hit anybody she liked with her cane.

They liked Frosty Flakes cereal, not icky eggs.

The dog's name was Sorrow and he ate scraps and didn't come inside the house.

There were four kittens and they slept in the barn.

School was okay.

Mackie sucked her thumb when no one was looking.

Mommy died a long time ago.

Emilie, reluctant to hear anything else, hurried them downstairs.

4

"YOU FIND OUT who she is, Matthew Michael Thomson. I'll not have a total stranger taking care of these children."

Matt took off his hat and wiped his dripping brow with his arm. The temperature was going to hit ninety today, most likely before noon, too. "Ruth, I told you. She was good to the girls in the store and she was looking for a job, a temporary job, until she decides if she's going back to graduate school or not. Now, quit waving that cane at me."

"If that woman's a college student, then I'm a rodeo champion," the woman snapped. "You see me wearing any fancy belt buckles like those bronc riders always strut around with?"

Matt saw a short, wide woman in a blue flowered dress resting her weight on a walnut cane. He couldn't help grinning down at her. "Ruthie, you'll always be a champion around here."

"Quit your teasing, Matthew. I want to know who that woman is."

"Ask her yourself."

"Since you can't tell me, then I guess I will. I don't like mysteries."

And Matt didn't like sticking his nose into other people's business. "She going to town with you?"

"No," Ruth grumbled. "She's staying home to make dinner."

That meant he wouldn't have to eat meat loaf again this Sunday. He swore his aunt made fifty-two at a time, one for each Sunday of the year. "And there's something wrong with that?"

"Not if she can cook, but if I was a wagering woman, I'd bet your new little housekeeper can't even pop corn."

Matt wasn't going to bet, either. He was running on optimism, faith and desperation right now. The combination could either turn deadly or save his skin. "Guess we'll have to wait and see then, won't we."

Ruth shrugged and started heading toward the three-room home that had once been the main farmhouse. "I'm going to go get dressed. I told your fancy new housekeeper to have the girls dressed and ready by nine."

"Then I'm sure it will be taken care of," Matt said, sure of no such thing. He worked outside for a few more hours. Despite the heat, there was a breeze from the south. It was a good morning to get some work done. He checked on the horses, talked to the men, replaced a couple of boards in the toolshed. He even started clearing out a space in the west shed for the new tractor. He'd forgotten what it was like to have a woman in the house. He'd been so surprised to see her up so early this morning that he'd hurried off as soon as he could.

Trying to keep out of everyone's way, he told himself. Oh, there was work to do. There was always work to do, but on Sundays he pretty much took it easy. The boys had kept up real well while he'd been gone, so there wasn't much else left to do but check on things that he'd already checked on.

He approached the kitchen door with reluctance. Emma Gray was a beautiful woman, the kind of woman that a rancher like himself should avoid like locusts. Once inside, he'd have to mind his manners and pretend he didn't notice how lovely she was. He was through with women, anyway.

Once inside, he'd probably have to start finding out more about the lady, ask for references, things like that. He'd hired a lot of men on a handshake and a gut feeling, though. Only once had he been wrong.

Still, Ruth was usually right about things, annoying as that was. Matt would hunt up Emma and have a little conversation, then he'd clean up for dinner. He couldn't wait for dinner. He hoped Emma could cook. Then maybe Ruth would calm down and realize that they'd managed to hold off Stephanie for a while longer and she should be grateful.

Matt opened the door and sniffed. Yep, smelled like food. Smelled like...smoke?

"WHAT THE HELL are you doing?"

Emilie jumped back from the stove, but didn't turn around. She knew whose voice the question belonged to and she was too busy to pay him any attention.

"You trying to burn the house down?" He came up beside her and turned one of the dials, shutting down the gas flames.

"I was trying to make dinner," she said, close to tears.

"I thought you said you could cook," Matt said.

She looked at him, then back to the slices of meat. "I've never cooked on a gas stove before. It's very...fast heat."

"We have gas because the power goes out a lot. At least with gas you can still cook a meal."

You could feel as if you were roasting in the flames of hell, too, Emilie thought. Heat blasted from the stove and there was no way air-conditioning could compete. "Would you move, please?"

He didn't budge. "You're burning whatever it is you're trying to cook."

"I'll scrape off the burned parts and start over."

"This isn't toast," he said. "You don't scrape meat."

"You do in Chicago." That seemed to shut him up. He moved aside while she stabbed the meat with a fork and put the charred pieces on a plate. It was a good thing the cast iron skillet started out black, because it was sure black now. "Why on earth don't you have nonstick pans in Nebraska?"

"Because we know how to cook," came the reply. She looked over her shoulder to see him looking at the opened cookbook.

"I know how to cook," she said. "I make an excellent Alfredo sauce."

"A what?"

"Never mind." She turned back to the stack of meat. Maybe if she baked it in water for a few weeks it would be edible. "Do you like pasta?"

"Not necessarily. I like meat. Sometimes chicken. And seafood when we go anywhere fancy, which isn't often." He reached over and took the plate of charred beef.

"What are you doing?" She really wondered if this time she was going to cry. It had taken her thirty minutes to find a recipe for Smothered Round Steaks and seven minutes to completely destroy the meat before she'd even had the chance to attempt the "smothered" part of the recipe.

"I'm going to give the dogs a thrill." He looked down at the meat. "Or indigestion."

"You can't give them our dinner. I told Mrs. Tuttle I would have dinner ready by one o'clock." She glanced at the clock above the refrigerator. "It's almost noon now. They'll be home soon."

"Make something else. There's enough beef in the freezers—you did find the freezers, didn't you?" She nodded. "There's enough beef downstairs to feed us for years. Thaw out some sirloin and fry up some steaks."

"I thought that was what I was doing."

"Round steak and sirloin aren't the same, honey," he drawled. "What else were you planning on having?"

"Green beans." She'd found cans of vegetables stacked on the basement shelves. "And rice." She knew how to do rice, thank goodness. He seemed to be waiting for her to continue. "Is there supposed to be more?"

"Rolls, pickles, dessert, and another vegetable. I'm partial to beets."

He could be partial to baked stuffed rattlesnakes, too, but that didn't mean she was cooking them. "Maybe this isn't going to work." Maybe she shouldn't have thought it could.

"It'll work. I'll go get the steaks, you stick that pan in the sink and get some water in it. We'll open the windows and get the smoke out before Ruth comes back. I'll help."

"You will? Why?"

"Because while we cook, you're going to tell me about yourself. And by the time Ruth gets home, she won't have to know that the new housekeeper burned the dinner."

Emilie couldn't help smiling a little. "She doesn't like me, does she?"

"Don't take it personally," Matt said, heading for the door. "She's still upset because she can't take care of the girls herself. She's angry because her hips ache and her doctor has her on a low-cholesterol diet."

"If she's worried about cholesterol, does that mean I shouldn't be cooking meat?"

"We're on a cattle ranch, Emma. That's what we've got. Meat."

"Oh." She grabbed a pot holder and moved the skillet into the sink as Matt left the kitchen. She squirted dishwashing liquid over the charred pieces that stuck to the bottom of the pan. She'd have to hide it so Mrs. Tuttle didn't see, because she didn't have the ten hours necessary to scrub the blasted thing clean. She filled it with hot water and stuck it in the oven, then crossed the room to open the windows above the sofa. You're going to tell me about yourself, he'd said.

No. She wasn't. It was too embarrassing to discuss with anyone. And until she gave her father time to come to his senses, she couldn't go home. And until she could go home, she had to support herself. And keep quiet.

"You sure made the dogs happy." Matt returned to the kitchen and dropped a pile of paper-wrapped packages on the counter.

"What are those?"

"Steaks. Thaw them out in the microwave and then we'll fry them."

"We will?"

He opened the door of the microwave and tossed the packages inside, then shut the door and started pushing buttons. "I figured I'd better help or we'll both have Ruth to answer to."

"Thank you."

"No problem." He turned back to her. "Do you know how to fry steaks?"

"Obviously not."

"First rule," he said, those dark eyes smiling down at her. "Don't have the heat turned up too high."

"Yes, I think I've learned that rule. What else should I do with these? A sauce? Sautéed veggies?"

"Worcestershire sauce or steak sauce is fine. Anything fancier than that is out. And we don't have 'veggies' in Nebraska." The microwave dinged, so

Matt reached in and rearranged the packages, then started it again.

"You sure know what you're doing."

The twinkle left his eyes. "I've had to."

Emilie knew enough to change the subject. "Have you always lived here, on this ranch?"

"Yeah. My great-grandparents settled this place. My grandfather added to it over the years so now it's one of the biggest ranches in the county."

"And you run it yourself?"

"I have help. Plenty of it."

And now he had her, who wasn't exactly starting off on the right track. How had she, Emilie Grayson, Chicago socialite and hostess extraordinaire, turned into a walking disaster zone? In a little over twenty-four hours she'd lost her fiancé, infuriated her father, walked out on her friends, and moved—temporarily, she consoled herself—to a remote area of Nebraska.

She didn't regret a thing. Emilie—no, Emma, she reminded herself—didn't have time to think about yesterday. Today she had dinner to cook.

Today she had a lot to learn. Especially before Ruth Tuttle returned.

"GREAT MEAL," Matt declared. "Can you pass the rice over here?"

She would pass him anything, as long as he kept

up the compliments. Emma lifted the heavy dish and managed to move it toward him. "Anything else?"

Ruth fussed with her food. "Wherever did you find this tablecloth?"

"In one of the drawers in the dresser," Emma replied. "Is there something wrong?"

"I guess not," she said, but she frowned at the thick white linen. "We don't usually get this fancy, not even on Sunday."

Matt lifted the platter of meat. "Seconds, anyone?"

Silence greeted that question. Emma supposed everyone was full. She turned to Mackie, who was seated beside her. "Would you like me to cut up some more of your meat for you?"

"No more, Emma," the child whispered, then yawned.

Ruth noticed. "These children are overtired, Matthew. You had no business keeping them out so late last night."

"It's a five-hour ride home, Aunt Ruth," he said, his voice mild. "And they had to get new clothes. You said so yourself."

She turned to Emma. "I heard you helped out with the shopping?"

"Yes. Would you like another helping of rice?"

"No, thank you all the same, I've had enough."

She made it sound as if she'd been poisoned, but Emma ignored her and kept a smile on her face. She wasn't her father's hostess for nothing and she'd dealt with far worse dinner guests. "Mrs. Tuttle, Matt said you grew up on this ranch. Has it changed much over the years?"

"More than a little." The old woman sighed. "We didn't have any of that fancy machinery then. My father and brothers worked with horses."

Mackie hopped down from her chair and crawled into her father's lap. He continued eating while he held her, which meant he'd had plenty of practice. Emma wondered if she had ever sat in her father's lap like that. She certainly didn't remember such a thing. She turned back to Matt's aunt. "How big a family did you have?"

"I was the only girl out of eight boys," she said with pride. "My father said I was more trouble than all eight boys put together."

Emma could believe that. "Were you the youngest?" She glanced toward Matt and saw that he had pushed his empty plate away and Mackie was sound asleep against his chest.

"I sure was. My momma used to say she wouldn't give up until she had a girl to help her in the kitchen."

Martha piped up, "I like to help in the kitchen."

Melissa agreed. "Me, too!"

"Would you help me clear the table?" The children nodded, so Emma stood up and began to remove the dirty plates by walking around the table the way she remembered their maid had done while the girls carried the smaller serving dishes. "Should I make coffee?"

"You should always make coffee," Ruth said. "Day and night, ranchers need their coffee. Remember that."

"I will." Hot coffee, undercooked meat, two kinds of vegetables. She was catching on to the rules.

"I'd rather have some more iced tea," Matt said. "I'd get it myself, but—"

"That's okay," Emma assured him, wishing she had six hands and an extra pair of legs. "I'll get the pitcher."

"You can just stack up the plates right here at the table," Ruth grumbled as Emma lifted her plate. "You're making a lot of work for yourself doing it like that."

Emma refused to let the old woman intimidate her. "This is a nicer way," she said.

"Where'd you say you was from?"

"Chicago." She put the dishes on the counter and picked up the iced tea pitcher. She went over to the table and refilled Matt's glass, then set the pitcher where he could reach it. Melissa dropped the salt shaker, which rolled under the table.

"I'll get it," she said, diving between the chairs. Emma walked carefully around the child's feet.

"Hmmmph. How'd you land in Lincoln, of all places? It's a nice little city and Lord knows we love that football team, but how—"

"Excuse me," Emma said, reaching in front of her for the platter of meat. There were only two steaks left, which had to be a sign that her dinner had been a success. She'd had her first lesson in frying, thanks to her employer, and she'd cooked her first meal. And people had eaten it, too. "Would anyone like ice cream? I found two kinds in the freezer, vanilla and strawberry."

"Me!" Melissa yelled, scooting backward on the floor. Emma tripped on the child's feet, the platter tipped, and the two chunks of meat zoomed like missiles toward Ruth Tuttle's wide bosom.

IT WAS THE BEST Sunday dinner ever, Martha declared. And, of course, her little sisters agreed. They hardly ever argued with her anyway and no one was going to deny seeing steaks fly. Mackie had woken with her father's shout in time to see Auntie Ruth jump up from the table. Melissa had scrambled to her knees and managed to look past Emma's waist as the meat went soaring into the air. Oh, it had been so much fun. They all agreed, sitting up in Martha's room where they had been sent to change out of their Sunday dresses, that this was more fun than the time Sorrow brought the mouse into the living room.

"Will Auntie Ruth make Emma go away?" Melissa asked.

"Nope." Martha slipped into her oldest cotton shorts. She grabbed her favorite purple T-shirt and pulled it over her head. "No way."

"You sure?"

"Yep. If she does, we'll just tell Mackie to cry and then Emma will stay. Right, Mackie?"

"Okay." Mackie sat on the floor and stuck her thumb in her mouth.

Melissa was out of her dress and into play clothes in a matter of seconds. "How long do we hafta stay up here?"

"Not long," Martha said, but she didn't want to say that she didn't know. Someone would have to put Mackie into bed for her nap. Martha wanted to take her Barbie dolls on the porch and play.

"Go ask," said Melissa.

"You."

"You're the oldest," the fraidy-cat returned.

"Okay," Martha said, going to the door. She listened for a second, but all was quiet downstairs. If Aunt Ruth was still talking, she could have heard it even all the way up here in the hall. Someone was coming up the stairs, though, so Martha didn't budge from her spot by the door. If there was anything going on, she wanted to be the first to hear it.

"Martha?" Emma appeared at the top of the stairs.

"Where's Mackenzie? Your father said she's supposed to take a nap every afternoon."

"She's in my room." Martha stepped back and opened the door wider. "She's supposed to go to the bathroom first."

"Okay. Where's that?"

"Right here." Martha led her to the small bathroom that divided her room from Mackie's.

Emma scooped Mackie from the floor without making her take her thumb out of her mouth the way Aunt Ruth would have. Martha followed Emma to make sure she did everything right. And she did, though Martha had to tell her that Mackie needed her three pink bears in the bed, too. And Mackie didn't have to wear pajamas at naptime, only at night.

"Is Aunt Ruth still in the kitchen?"

Emma's lips turned down. "No, she decided she had some things to do at home."

"Is she still mad?"

"Well, I don't know. I don't suppose she has ever had quite that kind of service before, do you?"

Martha stared up at her. "Don't feel bad, Emma. Daddy can give the meat to the dogs."

Emma smiled a funny upside-down smile. "If I keep this up, you'll have the happiest dogs in Nebraska."

Martha didn't understand, but she pretended to

look as if she did. When she went downstairs to clean up the mess, Martha and Melissa grabbed their boxes of dolls, furniture and clothes and headed downstairs to the screened porch. They would try not to make any noise, Martha reminded her sister.

If anything else funny happened today, Martha didn't want to miss it.

"HEARD YOUR FANCY new housekeeper threw food at Ruthie," Chet drawled from his prone position on a scarred leather couch. He pointed the remote at the television and the football game's volume went down a few decibel levels. The other three men in the bunkhouse groaned. "Sorry, boys," the old man said, "but I can't listen to two stories at the same time."

Matt pulled up an old metal chair and sat down. The room smelled of beer and cheese puffs. He'd stepped on a couple of those fat orange curls when he'd walked in. "She didn't throw the food. The plate slipped." The image would last in his mind forever.

"Ruth must have been ticked, though I'll bet it's not the first time someone's thrown something at her. Want a beer?"

Matt allowed himself a chuckle but kept the rest of his laughter tucked firmly in check. Chet was Ruth's cousin, the other three cowhands—Bobby, Jasper and Pete—her great-nephews or second cousins or something related in a way only Ruth could explain. Though their ages ranged from mid-forties to mid-fifties. Matt had always considered them uncles, taking the place of the father who had died too soon. Tall, lean and independent, with light hair and gray eyes, the Tuttles were good men who liked Ruth's meat loaf and apple pies. She doctored them when they were sick and scolded them when the animals got into her garden. None of the three had ever been married and it didn't look as if they ever intended to be. "I'll skip the beer, thanks. Didn't mean to barge in on the game. Just wanted you to know I bought that tractor. It'll be delivered sometime this week."

"Good." Chet nodded. "You going to keep the old one around or sell it?"

"I haven't decided yet. What do you think? I could probably sell it to Barney, but I'd kinda hate to see it go." Matt stretched his legs out in front of him and eyed the television. The Patriots were ahead of the Bears, but it looked like a good game. And the bunk-house was the safest place to be right now. Matt grinned, thinking of Sunday dinner. He'd had all he could do to keep from falling off his chair when he'd seen Emma's face after the sirloins hit their unintentional target.

Chet shrugged. "I'm partial to the old gal."

Matt wondered if the old man was talking about

the tractor or Aunt Ruth. "Yeah," was all he could safely say.

"What's her name?"

Matt scooped up a handful of cheese curls from the opened bag on the table. "Who?"

"The new housekeeper. You going to bring her around to meet everyone or are you afraid she'll throw stuff at us, too?"

"We're shakin' in our boots," Bobby, the youngest at forty-six, declared. "Is she good-looking?"

"She's not half bad." Matt kept his gaze on the television screen. He would spend some time here in the bunkhouse watching the game. He'd had about all the female companionship one man could take for one weekend.

Chet hit the remote again and the volume rose just in time for the next play. Pete turned around and winked at his boss. "Just what we need around here, another female."

"Uh-oh." Jasper swore. "Chicago just made first down."

"You should marry again," the old man suggested. "Have yourself a son."

Matt shook his head. "I think I'm out of the marrying business, Chet. The women in Nebraska are safe from me."

"You just brought another one home," Chet said.

"One that's not 'half bad,' you say? Ruth says she's too fancy for the sand hills."

Jasper chuckled. "You talking about the woman or the tractor?"

Matt ignored the question. "Ruth's probably right, but I didn't have a whole lot of choices." He sat back in his chair and studied the television screen as if he'd never seen a football game before. Matt cleared his throat and ignored the men's curious looks. "Think the Patriots will get to the Superbowl again this year?"

He sure wasn't going to talk about his beautiful new steak-throwing housekeeper any longer.

5

THERE WAS NO DISHWASHER. No matter how hard she searched, no machine appeared behind cabinet doors. The dishes would be washed by hand—her hands—and stacked and dried and put away.

It took a long while and by the time she was done, her forehead was coated with perspiration and her fingertips were shriveled. The image of Ruth Tuttle picking meat from her lap did little to make Emma think that her days here would be happy ones. She'd promised Matt that she would stay long enough for him to advertise again for a housekeeper. It was going to feel like a very long time if food kept flying at the Thomson relatives. Something told her that Mrs. Tuttle wouldn't forget that incident very quickly.

Still, she reminded herself, this was better than going home. She'd choose Matt's aunt's wrath over her father's any day. She wiped the countertops clean, left the tablecloth on the table for tonight, and decided she'd better check on the girls. Last time she'd seen them, they were on their way to the front porch to play.

The Thomson house was one of those picturesque Victorian homes that Emma would expect to see in a movie about ranches in the Midwest. She explored each room downstairs. The kitchen, which she was only too happy to leave, led to a living room that took up half the house. There was a brick fireplace on one end, windows that opened on to the screened porch on the other. Close to the fireplace were built-in bookcases; nearby sat a dust-covered round oak table and four chairs. Emma walked past an oversize tan sofa with matching chairs that faced an oak entertainment center. The shades were pulled against the afternoon sun, but Emma found the thermostat and turned the air conditioner to a lower temperature. Housework, she was discovering, was hot work.

The front door led to the porch, where the girls could be heard talking to each other. The windows were closed on the porch, so even this area was cooled by central air. The view from the door showed the long drive to the main road and a cluster of leafy trees, from one of which hung a rope swing. All in all, a comfortable place, although it seemed empty. Maybe the ranch was quiet every Sunday.

"Hi," Emma said, entering the porch where the girls played. She stepped hesitantly closer to the wide expanse of Barbie dolls and pink plastic furniture. "You look like you're having fun."

"Yep," Melissa said, holding up a doll dressed in an elaborate bride costume. "Wanna play?"

"Sure." She sat down cross-legged on an empty spot near them. Melissa handed her a white-gowned Barbie doll. "You can be the bride."

"No, thanks. Can I be something else, like a bridesmaid?" She spotted a naked doll in the midst of a pile of clothes. "How about a cowgirl?"

Martha shrugged. "You can dress her any way you want. We're having a wedding and she can be the best friend."

"Best friends can be very helpful at weddings," Emma said, thinking of Paula. She would have to call her soon and find out what had happened at the church after she'd left. That was, if she really wanted to know.

Maybe she would be better off not hearing the gruesome details. Ken would have left quietly after having given a brief statement to the press. Her father would say she'd been taken ill, of course. The truth would be, as Ken had so succinctly put it, "political suicide." Going through with the marriage would have been disastrous for her, politically advantageous for Ken. She wondered what Matt would think about her if he knew she had run away from her own wedding.

She didn't think he'd understand.

"Emma?"

"What?"

Martha stared at her with an odd expression. "Are you married?"

"No."

"Do you have a boyfriend?"

"Not anymore."

The child smiled, her heart-shaped face lighting up with happiness. "Good." She handed her the Barbie with the white dress and flowing tulle veil. "Then you can be the bride since you're the oldest."

Emma took the doll and pretended to be honored. "Is there a groom around here?"

"Yep, but his head keeps coming off. See if it's in the Corvette."

"Let's just have a headless groom," Emma said, feeling more cheerful. "Trust me. Barbie's not going to care."

"She's not?" Melissa looked doubtful.

"Absolutely not. Do you think she really wants to get married?"

The girls nodded. "Yes," Martha said. "She likes the dress."

Emma smiled, thinking of her own wasted gown. If she'd spent less time planning an elaborate wedding and more time paying attention to her fiancé's behavior, she might have saved herself and everyone around her a lot of trouble. "Fair enough," she told the little girls. "Let's pretend that Barbie is in a movie and only pretending to get married."

"I like that," Martha agreed. "She can marry Tom Cruise."

"Absolutely," Emma said, though she preferred Harrison Ford any day. Matthew Thomson looked a little like Harrison, now that she thought about it. He had a handsome face that looked a little beat-up, lived-in and comfortable. A man of strength and action, he was not the kind of man who would deceive his own bride to suit his purposes.

Then again, what did she know about men? Her judgment wasn't exactly faultless these days. "How many brides are we going to have in our movie?"

"Three," Martha declared. "We'll take turns."

"Fair enough," Emma said, holding her doll upright on the floor. She had never in twenty-six years played dolls like this. It was almost worth having to wash all those dishes.

"WE'VE GOT ourselves some company." Chet hauled himself off the couch as he saw the little girls approaching the bunkhouse. Matt sighed. There were four people heading in this direction and one of them was the oddest employee he'd ever hired.

"You want me to head them off or do you want to meet Emma?"

The men voted to meet Emma. Bobby brushed his

hair back, Jasper tucked in his shirt and Pete set his beer bottle in the sink where it wouldn't be seen. Chet stood by the window and waved at the girls. "Holy mackerel, Matt, but she's a looker, all right."

"She's not half bad," Matt conceded, knowing full well that Emma looked like a model or a movie star. She had the kind of skin that made a man wonder how women could be that soft and delicate. "She can't cook for beans, though."

Jasper looked at him as if he were nuts. "Cook? Why should she have to cook?"

"Because I hired her as a housekeeper, a mother to the girls, a cook."

"You went and got yourself a wife," Pete muttered. "She'll have you eating out of her hand in no time at all."

"I'm not planning on spending much time with her," Matt protested. "You guys are making too much of this."

"Yeah, sure," Pete chuckled. He opened the door when Martha banged on it. "Why, lookee who's here come to visit her old uncles?"

Martha grinned. "Hi, Uncle Pete. Is Daddy here?"

"Yes, ma'am, he sure is." Pete stepped back and let the three children and their companion step inside the room. "We were watching Chicago get beat pretty bad. Howdy, ma'am," he said to Emma. "Name's Pete Larkin. Pleased to meet you."

Emma shook hands with all the men, while Matt stood by and watched the show. His ranch hands acted as if they had women stop by the bunkhouse every Sunday afternoon. Jasper fixed her a soda, Pete gave her the best spot on the couch, Bobby hovered nearby with the bag of cheese puffs and Chet kept smiling at her as if she were the Queen of England.

"Daddy, will you take us on a tractor ride? Please?" Melissa wrapped her arms around his legs and looked up at him with those pleading eyes. Mackie was beside her, with an identical expression on her face while Martha hung back and listened to Emma's conversation with Chet.

"It's pretty hot out there," he said, hoping to dissuade her. "Maybe tomorrow."

"That's what you always say."

"The new tractor isn't here yet. It's just the old one, Mel."

"That's okay. Emma wanted to see the ranch, so we told her that you would take her for a ride on the tractor. You will, won't you?"

"Yeah," Chet said, winking at him. "You will, Matthew. The lady ought to have some idea of where she's working." He turned to Emma. "Have you ever been on a cattle ranch before, hon?"

"No. Never."

"Bet you've never been out of the city, either," the old man declared. He grinned at Matt. "You'd better show her the ropes, son. You've had a hard enough time finding some help, so you'd better treat this one right."

Matt refrained from pointing out that he'd cooked today's dinner, which was pretty good treatment right there.

"This is what you call the sand hills?" Emma asked.

"Yes, ma'am. The Great Plains. It's God's country, ma'am, and no doubt about it."

"Please call me Emma." She smiled at all four men and Matt wondered if they'd ever be the same again. They stood there like four silly lumps of clay, grinning as if they had nothing better to do than flirt with the new housekeeper. Which they didn't, because it was their day off, too.

"All right," Matt said, his voice gruff. "Let's go for that tractor ride."

"Emma, too?" Martha asked.

"Emma, too. If she wants."

Her face lit up and she smiled at him. He swore the temperature in the bunkhouse went up ten degrees. "I've never ridden on a tractor before."

"Well, here's your big chance," he said, knowing he was stuck entertaining the woman. He put his Stetson on his head and stopped in front of the air conditioner in the east window. He turned the fan higher. No reason to suffer on one of the last hot days of the season.

"Goody!" Mackie ran up to him and stuck her hand in his. "I had a nap," she whispered. "And I didn't wet the bed."

"Good for you," he said automatically.

"I didn't wear a diaper, either," she confided. "I'm a big girl now. Martha said."

Martha was the self-appointed expert of big-girlness. "Then it must be true." He turned to Emma as they left the bunkhouse. "You want a hat?"

She shook her head. "I'm fine."

She'd have heatstroke in thirty minutes, so Matt turned back to the house and retrieved a battered old Stetson that had belonged to another visitor. He stuck it on Emma's head. "You'd better wear this. You're not used to this kind of heat and you don't want to get heatstroke on your first day."

"Thanks." She didn't look convinced, but she left the hat on her head even though the brim slipped over her eyes. "I feel like a real cowgirl now."

She sure as hell didn't look like one, not even though she wore jeans and a T-shirt. Her sneakers were new, her socks white, and she wore pink lipstick as if she were going to town. "You're going to have to get dirty to look like a cowhand," he told her. "Come on. I'll show you the barn."

"Goody," one of the girls said. "We can see the kittens."

"The girls aren't allowed out here unless there's an adult with them," Matt told his new housekeeper. "There's too much equipment, too many animals, too much that can go wrong if they're in the wrong place at the wrong time. If they want to play they can do it in the front yard."

"Where the swing is," Emma said.

"Yeah. I've got men coming and going in trucks, motorcycles and on horseback. They don't need to be watching out for children while they're doing their work. The bunkhouses are off-limits to women, too. If you need someone from out there, use the phone. There's a list of numbers in the kitchen by the telephone. The men are entitled to their privacy."

"I understand. Women and children stay in the house where they belong."

He couldn't have put it better, though he suspected she was teasing him. "Yeah. Easy enough."

"Easy enough," she agreed. "I won't get in anyone's way. And I intend to hide from your aunt, too."

Matt looked down at the woman who was matching him stride for stride. "She'll get over it, you know. She might even think it's funny."

"No, I don't think so." Emma looked up at him. "I'm not fired for that?"

"Melissa tripped you, that's all. Accidents happen." *Accidents happen.* How he hated that phrase, and here he'd gone and used it himself. "You'll do fine. By the time Ruth washes her dress, she'll have forgotten all about it."

"You don't really believe that."

"Well..." No, he really didn't, but he didn't want Emma leaving the job the first day. He needed her, no matter how bad a cook she was. She was better than nothing at this point, and he was prepared to overlook a few flaws. They approached the shed that was attached to the largest barn.

"Here's what we call the big barn." He pointed north. "The little barn is over there, along with some of the sheds for calving and also the place where we do some of our own doctoring."

"What's that?" Emma pointed to a small group of houses.

"One of them belongs to Ruth, the others are housing for the summer workers and one is an extra place I use on nights when I don't have time to clean up and come inside the house. During calving season, for instance. I keep an extra bunk in there, plus there's a television with cable for the weather station."

"This is a big place," she said, holding Melissa's hand.

Martha squeezed in between them. "Can we ride the tractor first?"

"Yes, honey. You wait here and let me get it started up." He had the old beast roaring in no time, though the engine needed more work and the clutch stuck. He hitched up a hay wagon and let all four of them climb on. "Hang on," he told them. "Emma, don't let Mackie close to the edge."

She tucked the child in her lap and put her arms around her. Once Matt was sure that everyone was ready, he took them along the road to the north buildings. They waved to Bobby, who came out of the bunkhouse to get another bag of groceries from his pickup. They swung in a loop around the little barn and headed over the hill. He would give her a view of the sand hills, Matt decided. He would let her see what kind of country she had landed in. The grass, golden green and moving in the wind, was over a foot high. Here and there the Angus cattle wandered with their calves. Matt put the tractor in neutral and turned to his passengers. "Watch out for rattlesnakes," he said, and watched Emma turn pale.

"We won't get out of the wagon," she promised, scrambling to her feet. "We'll just look from here, right, Mackie?" Mackie nodded.

He drove them around for a while more, past the hill where a cavalry scout had been attacked by Indians, past a cemetery where several of his ancestors were buried. The noisy tractor didn't give him much chance to talk, which was fine. By the time he returned them to the barn, he'd run out of things to say.

Matt helped the girls jump off the wagon bed, but of course Emma took his hand, too, as if she were accepting it for a turn around a dance floor. She tripped getting out of the wagon and fell smack-dab against him.

"Oh!" she said, balancing herself by grabbing his arm with her free hand. "I'm sorry. These new sneakers—"

"No problem," he managed to reply, though his body burned from the brief contact. Her breasts had been soft against his chest and her thighs had grazed his in a very disturbing way when she'd slid against him to stand on the ground. He looked down at her shoes. "They're not going to stay white for long."

She shrugged and backed up a step. Matt told himself he was relieved. "They're comfortable and that's what counts." She turned to the girls. "Come on, ladies. Baths before supper!"

He watched as she admired the kittens the girls had scooped up to show her. He had work to do, but he couldn't remember what.

He had no right to be attracted to her. No reason, either, except she was a beauty with a charming innocence who cried real tears and seemed to genuinely enjoy the children. No, he had no reason to be attracted to her. If he was looking for a wife, he would pick from several local women. Women who knew what this life was like, who didn't expect their husbands to wear suits and ties and work from nine till five.

He'd made that mistake before, marrying Stephanie's Omaha friend. The girls' mother. The woman who had driven away without so much as a backward glance and had gotten herself killed on Interstate 80 during a thunderstorm.

Doctors had managed to save the baby, leaving Matt with an infant, a toddler and a four-year old to raise. He'd been riddled with grief and guilt, a combination guaranteed for sleepless nights. He couldn't have slept anyway, not with Mackie awake every four hours needing a bottle.

No, he had no business liking this city woman, or wondering what that skin would feel like if he touched it with his fingers.

He would make a practical choice next time, for his girls needed a mother and he needed, well, he needed some female companionship of a different sort. He hadn't had sex since he'd conceived MacKenzie. He didn't go for one-night stands; and anything he did in town would be public knowledge and widely gossiped about. He didn't cotton to being the subject of anyone's gossip.

So he was ready for a woman. He should never have hired such a beautiful one. He was getting distracted. He was thinking thoughts he shouldn't think.

He was thinking about taking another cold shower.

Darn it, Ruth was right. It was about time he started thinking about getting married again. There were several nice women in the county. Available women who knew how to live with a rancher, who knew that a new tractor was more important than a new station wagon or that trip to Hawaii.

Matt turned and checked on his four passengers, but his gaze rested on Emma. She was laughing and so were his daughters. The lady wasn't hard to look at, but she was no ranch wife.

THEY WERE GOING to expect to be fed again. Emma pulled her hair back into a short ponytail and stood closer to the vent where cool air entered the living room. In a few minutes she was going to have to face that kitchen and turn on that heat-producing beast of a stove. Even worse, she was going to have to cook something on it.

"Emma?"

She turned to see Martha looking at her. "What?"

"What are you doing?"

Emma stepped away from the wonderful vent and put her hands on her hips. "Thinking about dinner."

"We could have Jell-O," Martha said. "Aunt Stephanie makes lots of Jell-O."

"Where does Aunt Stephanie live?" Next door, hopefully, so she would be able to provide tips and recipes.

"She lives in Omaha."

"Oh." So much for a support system. "How do you make Jell-O?"

"With water, that's all."

"Good." Come to think of it, making Jell-O looked easy on those television commercials. "Let's go see if we have any. It comes in little boxes, right?"

"Right." Martha followed her into the kitchen.

"Where are Mel and Mackie?"

"They're playing upstairs."

They were dancing, of course. After the tractor ride, they'd had lemonade and then decided to wear their ballet slippers and practice twirling. Martha still wore hers. "I like the black leggings, but aren't you hot?"

The child shook her head. "I look like a dancer. They always wear long T-shirts over their leggings. They never care if they're hot. I saw it in a book."

"No wonder I didn't make a good ballet dancer." Emma looked at her watch. Supper was to be at six, an hour from now, and she had no idea what to do for an encore. She had no idea what to do each night for the next two weeks.

"You know how to dance like a ballerina?"

"A little bit." Everyone at Miss Keaton's Academy took ballet.

"Wow."

"We'll dance later," she promised, and hoped she could remember the beginning steps. Ballet sounded like more fun than struggling in the kitchen. "For now, we have to make Jell-O."

"I like orange the best."

Emma led her into the kitchen. "Then let's hope we have orange."

They found two boxes and followed the directions, then poured the orange liquid into soup bowls and refrigerated them. Martha chattered throughout the entire process, filling Emma in on second-grade society and the fact that her teacher was going to have a baby. Emma interrupted her only once, to ask what they usually ate for supper on Sunday nights.

"Leftovers," the child said.

The only leftovers had smacked Ruth in the chest, so reheated steaks were not an option. "I don't think we have any."

Martha put her hands on her hips. "Don't you know how to cook anything?"

"Of course I do." She knew how to make three different romantic dinners for two. She could scramble eggs and make toasted cheese sandwiches, but she was better at meal planning than she was at meal making. The Graysons' cook had never complained, but then again Mrs. LaTour made a good salary with health benefits, stock options and four weeks vacation in France each year. Her kitchen was her domain and her employers were not invited inside. She would not have welcomed assistance with the Jell-O.

"Does your father like pasta?"

The child looked blank.

"Pasta," Emilie repeated. "Spaghetti. Noodles. Macaroni."

Martha nodded. "Oh, sure. Spaghetti's cool."

Thank goodness there were two boxes in the cupboard, and she'd seen the other ingredients in the bins in the refrigerator. This time she wasn't going to embarrass herself in front of Matt Thomson. She was going to earn her salary, because when she was through with her first job she was going to spend a month in Europe. Which is where she should have gone in the first place, though what she would have done in Paris without her credit cards she had no idea.

She thought of her oddly appealing rancher. No, she wouldn't leave just yet. No, Matt Thomson needed her. Needed her help. And at the rate she was going marriage-wise, this might be her only chance to have a family for a long time.

She'd thought she would be a good mother. She'd expected to have children, though Ken had never been enthusiastic about the subject of having a family. She'd known he was preoccupied with his career. She'd known he'd expected her by his side—as his hostess and as his asset.

And now she didn't have to be either. Now she was Emma Gray and she didn't even have to dress up for dinner.

6

"WHAT IS THIS?"

"Pasta primavera," Emma announced, setting the plate in front of Matt. "One of my specialties." It was actually her one and only specialty, but she wasn't going to tell him that. He didn't need to know that she'd always lived in a house with its own cook.

"I see." He poked at it with his fork. "Where's the meat?"

"It's a vegetable dish." Which she thought would have been obvious, considering the broccoli florets and julienne carrots atop the pasta. "Martha helped me make it."

"Well," he said, turning to study his oldest daughter. "How did you do that?"

"I washed things," the child said. "And I found the spaghetti and I set the table."

Emma finished serving the girls. "I hope you like it."

"We made a surprise for dessert, too," Martha leaned forward and whispered. "You can't guess, either."

"I wouldn't even try," her father said.

"It's better with freshly grated parmesan, but all I could find was this can." Emma sprinkled cheese on the girls' pasta and then handed it to Matt before she sat down. "Ladies, napkins in your laps, please." They did as they were told without complaint.

Matt glanced at Melissa and Mackenzie, then looked back at them again. "What on earth are you wearing?"

"Ballet outfits."

"Actually they're wearing tights and shirts, because they have their new ballet shoes on and—"

Matt frowned at her. "They're wearing my undershirts."

"They said you wouldn't mind."

He gulped. "Next time you girls have to ask me first."

They nodded, undisturbed. There was silence as the four Thomsons contemplated their vegetable-covered spaghetti.

"You don't like it?" Emma's heart sank. She'd counted on this dish to impress her employer.

"It's not that I don't like it." Matt speared a broccoli floret and twirled spaghetti onto his fork. "I've just never had it before." He gave her what she hoped was a reassuring smile. He didn't smile much, so that was a good sign. "It looks good. Real colorful here on the plate."

"We set a place for Ruth." Of course, that spot was empty. "I guess I scared her off."

"She usually doesn't come here at night," Matt assured her. "She likes to watch the news and talk back to Dan Rather."

"She watches 'Wheel of Fortune,'" Melissa piped up. "We all do. Vanna's pretty."

"No television on school nights," their father said. He looked across the table to Emma. "We're going into town for a barbecue tomorrow. You're welcome to come along if you want. There's a big crowd and always room for one more. The profits go to the community center."

She'd almost forgotten about the long weekend and Monday holiday. On Monday she and her new husband were to have arrived in Paris to begin a three-day honeymoon. Anything longer would have taken too much time away from the election; anything less would have made Ken look too politically minded and overconcerned with his own career, her father had explained. "Thank you for the invitation, but I think I'll stay here."

"You should take the day off," he insisted. "Since you worked all day today."

"How far away is town?"

"Blindon's about fifteen minutes north of here. It's a small place, but it has a little bit of everything. Groceries, doctor, feed store, JCPenney catalogue store. And it's where the girls go to school."

"And the café!" Martha reminded him. "With the best chocolate shakes in the whole world."

Emma raised her eyebrows in mock horror. "Better than at Grandma's Good Eats in Lincoln?"

"Stu's," Matt explained. "And she's right. You should go with us, so I can show you where Mackie's preschool is. If you make a list of groceries, we can get those, too."

"Groceries?" Emma now knew she'd gone too far. Next thing she knew he'd expect her to change the tires on the station wagon.

"Have you looked in the pantry to see what you need?"

She needed a cook. She needed a maid. And she needed a couple of aspirin. "Um, not yet. I'll do that tonight." Right before she called Paula for help.

"We'll leave at one," Matt said, as if the plans for tomorrow were settled. He looked down at his plate and sighed. "This sure would be good if it had a little meat in it."

"Do you have any idea what's going on here?"

Emma stretched out the telephone cord and dragged a kitchen chair over to the wall. "No, Paula, of course I don't. I've been busy and you'll never believe—"

"Pick up a newspaper," her friend shrieked. "You've made the tabloids and your father has locked himself in the house and refused to make statements except to say that you're ill and he's praying for a speedy recovery. Ken's sisters have been hustled off to the lake for the long weekend so they won't be available to the press. No one knows where Ken is, but Fred thinks he and some of his friends are fishing. Or saying they are."

"I guess it was too much to hope that this would die down."

"Just a little, darling." Paula sighed. "Where on earth are you? Wherever you are, I hope you're able to stay there."

"How ill am I supposed to be?"

"Very ill. Mentally and or physically. Your father is hinting about a nervous breakdown, but of course cannot come out and say you are flawed in any way. Mentally unbalanced brides make terrible senators' wives."

"If you could see me now you'd wonder about my sanity," Emma whispered. She wore a faded blue housedress that she'd found in her closet and her feet were bare. The house was quiet; the children were in bed and Matt was still outside, though the sky had grown dark. "I can't talk for long, but I wanted to—"

"Emilie, tell me where you are. I wouldn't be surprised if your father has hired private detectives to find you. He can't go on saying you're ill forever. Are you safe?''

''Very.''

''Can I tell him you called?''

''No, I don't think you'd better. I told him I would call him in a few days, and I will.''

''He'll trace the call, you know,'' Paula warned. ''He's furious about your running away. He was very icy and polite to me afterward. When the minister announced that the wedding had been postponed you would have thought he'd announced that we'd just been invaded by aliens. The press is having a field day.''

''He canceled my credit cards.''

''To force you home? That makes sense.''

''No, he threatened to disown me if I didn't marry Ken, and I suppose he means what he said.''

''Impossible. Even George Grayson isn't capable of doing that. He'll calm down in a few days.'' Paula's voice rose a notch. ''Lunch on Monday? Where? No, dear, not there. Last time I ate at Mario's the place was so noisy I couldn't hear myself talk.''

''Fred's home?''

''Oh, yes, absolutely. Hold on, darling.'' She heard Paula talk to her husband, then Paula came back on the line. ''He's gone into the shower, so we have plenty of time to talk. If you have no credit cards, then where are you?"

"I have a job."

Silence. "A job?" her friend echoed. "You?"

"Yes. A real job."

"Good," Paula declared. "It's about time you had a life separate from George Grayson. What are you doing and how did you find something so quickly?"

"I was shopping," Emma explained, though she was reluctant to tell Paula that she was cooking and baby-sitting on a ranch. "And one thing led to another."

"You always were an excellent shopper."

"It came in handy," she said, thinking of the frustrated expression on Matt's face when he'd stood in the middle of the girls' clothing department. "I'm enjoying being on my own, Paula."

"Should I wire money?"

She hesitated. Paula would send her anything she asked, but that wasn't right, either. She had a roof over her head, a place to sleep and food to eat. As long as she fixed it herself, she thought wryly. "No, I'm fine. I have everything I need right here."

"I'm tempted to believe you."

"You should. I really am fine."

Paula sighed again. "You didn't deserve this, Emmy. Ken behaved badly."

"Yes." Emma didn't really want to get into that

subject. "He wouldn't have been happy married to me."

"Sure he would." Paula snorted. "It would have made him look like a prince." Her friend sighed. "You'll let me know if you need anything?"

"I promise. I'm going to give you my phone number, just in case there's an emergency with my father and I need to come home." She recited the numbers into the phone. "Don't give this number to anyone."

"What area code is 402?"

"Nebraska."

"Nebraska," Paula repeated, her voice faint. "How did you end up there?"

Emma looked around the kitchen that she'd just spent an hour cleaning. "Just lucky, I guess."

THIS WAS A terrible idea. He shouldn't have brought Emma with him. Her very presence was going to put a cramp in any chance he had to look around for a woman to date. Matt led his family and his guest through the crowd at the annual Blindon barbecue and hoped that no one would notice the beautiful woman holding hands with his youngest daughters as if she were part of the family.

"This is a terrible idea," Ruth grumbled, leaning on her cane. "That woman has no business being here. What are people going to think?"

"That I hired some help." He kept his expression

deliberately bland. People were going to think that he'd gotten over the death of his wife and had brought home a woman to sleep with. The women in town were going to pretend to be shocked and the men in town were going to wonder how he managed such a feat, and both sexes would just about drown themselves in curiosity over the Triple Creek sleeping arrangements.

"You get some strange ideas in your head, boy. Bringing home a stranger who can't cook for beans, for one thing. Melissa told me they ate orange Jell-O for breakfast this morning."

"It was supposed to be last night's dessert, but it hadn't set yet." Much to the disappointment of his new housekeeper. He'd had a hard time keeping a straight face when she and Martha had tried to serve orange-flavored water for last night's dessert.

Ruth glared at two teenaged boys who were in her way. The boys moved quickly, their eyes on the cane that Ruth wielded like a sword. "You shouldn't have hired a baby-sitter who looks like a movie star. People are gonna talk."

"Let them," he said, watching the curve of Emma's bottom. The teenaged boys were, too, though this time they were safely away from striking distance of Ruth's cane.

"Easy for you to say," she sniffed. "Everyone will be asking me what's going on."

"You can tell them I'm thinking of dating again. Thought I'd ask Gerta Lapinski out to dinner."

Ruth stopped in her tracks and glared up at him. "Haven't you got enough trouble?"

"I thought you liked Gerta. Isn't her mother in one of your clubs?"

"Gerta Lapinski doesn't have a maternal bone in her body." Ruth glanced around as if to see who was listening. "She's more interested in her job at the bank."

"There's nothing wrong with that." Matt liked Gerta. She'd approved his loan for the new tractor.

"There is if you have three daughters to raise," Ruth sniffed. "And you're going to want sons, too."

"I don't think I have much say in the matter."

Ruth nodded toward the long tables piled high with food where a group of women stood serving the meal. "What about Corinne Linden? She's a lovely woman who didn't deserve a no-good husband like Larry Linden, if you ask me."

Corinne Linden was a quiet blonde who had two teenaged sons, one of whom had been staring at Emma's rear a minute ago, and a mean ex-husband who tended to show up looking for trouble whenever he returned to town. "I'll talk to her," Matt promised. But he didn't elaborate on what he'd say.

Ruth was warming to the subject. "Don't forget

Alice Peters, either. She's never been married, though she might be a little young for you."

"I'm only thirty-six, Ruth. Alice has to be at least thirty by now." Alice was short, plump, cheerful and kind. He'd known her most of his life, and he liked her well enough, but she'd never treated him like anything other than a big brother. And he'd never thought of her as anything more than a casual friend.

"That Emma person is trouble. If I were you, I'd send her back to where she came from."

Matt abandoned all pretense of calm and stared down at his aunt. "And then what? Give the children to Stephanie to raise? Is that really what you want?"

Ruth's eyes filled with tears. "You know I don't, Matthew. I love those girls and they belong with their father."

"Then be nice to Emma, because for now she's the only person keeping the kids at home. If I don't have help—"

"Or remarry," Ruth interjected.

"I can't do it alone," he concluded, still frowning. He turned to see where his family had gone. Ruth tapped the toe of his boot with her cane until he turned back to her.

"I'll try," she promised. "I really will try to be nice."

"That would help." Matt wondered how long Ruth would keep her word. He looked around for

Emma and his daughters and saw them standing by the runza booth. "I'm going to mingle," he said. "Do you want something to eat?"

She shook her head. "I'm going to find the Garden Club and see what I can do to help. If there are any rumors, I'll hear 'em there first and maybe I can stop a few." She looked past him to where Emma stood talking to a young cowhand. "You'd better guard your territory or you'll lose a housekeeper faster than you can say 'mating season.'"

Matt moved quickly through the crowd until he stood next to Emma. Her head barely came to his shoulder, but she looked up at him and smiled. "Mr. Trowbridge was explaining what a runza is."

Hal Trowbridge removed his cowboy hat, exposing a white forehead and curly black hair. "Call me Hal, ma'am."

"Hello, Hal. Heard you had a good summer out at the Bar X." Matt moved his hand to Emma's elbow in a protective gesture that the young man recognized right away.

"Yessir, sure did." He put his hat back on and took a few steps backward. "Hope you have a good time today, ma'am," were his parting words before he spun on his heels and disappeared into the crowd.

"You scared him," Emma complained.

"If you're looking for a boyfriend, Hal's too young for you."

"I'm not looking for a boyfriend." She laughed, which made his daughters giggle. "I can't imagine anything I need less."

"Women always say that," he muttered, and pulled his wallet from his jeans pocket. "We'll take five runzas, thanks," he told the woman across the table.

Emma took the triangle of pastry wrapped in wax paper. "Am I going to like this?"

"Sure. Why wouldn't you?"

Martha squirted some ketchup on hers. "Everyone loves them, Emma. They're yummy."

"Yummy," Mackie repeated, while Melissa got carried away with a yellow dispenser and squirted mustard all over her pink shirt. Emma reached for a napkin and attempted to clean up the mess while Matt paid for the food and collected his change. They looked like one big happy family, he thought, except that Melissa was crying and Emma had just knelt on the child's fallen runza.

Matt bought another runza, gave it to Melissa and then herded his family to an empty picnic table. Emma eyed her lunch suspiciously. "It smells good, but what's in it?"

"Meat and cabbage."

"Oh."

He grinned at the hesitant expression on her face.

"Try it and if you don't like it I'll get you a hamburger."

She bit delicately into the dough and chewed for a moment. After swallowing, she looked surprised. "It's really very good."

Matt nodded. "We'll make a Nebraskan out of you eventually."

"Stranger things have happened, I suppose. Tell me the name of the football team again?"

"Cornhuskers," Martha announced.

"Please, do not speak while you have food in your mouth."

"I'll get some drinks," Matt offered, suddenly feeling a little too comfortable. He had no business smiling at his housekeeper and acting like, well, like he thought she was beautiful. He left the table to buy some root beers and talk about the price of corn with some of the other men who had taken the afternoon off to be with their families. He'd keep an eye out for young men who buzzed around Emma, though. He hadn't brought her to Blindon to find herself a husband.

When he returned with the drinks and set them on the table, Emma smiled up at him. "This is really fun, Matt. Thank you for asking me."

He looked down into those pretty green eyes and his heart dropped to his belly. Somehow he didn't think he'd be getting around to asking Gerta Lapinski to dinner.

"SHOW EMMA MY SCHOOL," Martha pleaded. She hung over the seat of the truck and made sure she talked into her father's right ear. She wanted to make sure he showed Emma everything in town, because she didn't want to go home yet. Daddy would go outside and not come back until dark and Emma would try to cook something weird and make everyone take baths.

"I'm heading that way," her father said. "Sit back down, Martha, and put your seat belt on."

She obeyed, but not before she saw Emma drawing something on the back of an envelope. "What are you writing, Emma?"

"I'm drawing a map and taking notes about where you all go to school. And at what times."

"I love school," Melissa said softly. "I wish I went all day instead of kindergarten."

"Mackie doesn't go tomorrow, does she?"

"No," her father said. "Tomorrow's Tuesday."

"She gets to stay home with Emma." Martha wondered what they would do all morning. Make more Jell-O? Play dolls? She knew they would have fun.

"But I pick up Melissa at kindergarten at twelve. And then we'll do the grocery shopping together. I think we're all too tired to bother with that today."

Emma turned around and smiled at Martha. "And you come home at three o'clock on the school bus, right?"

"Will you be home?" Suddenly it was terribly important that Emma say yes.

"Of course. Where else would I be?"

She didn't know, but she really really wanted Emma to stay on the ranch. Martha wished she could remember her mother. She was sure her mother would have been waiting for her after school. She would have cookies ready, like Jennifer's mother did. She would smell good and she would know all of the answers to Martha's questions. A mother would want to see all of her papers and would kiss her and hug her when she walked in the door.

Martha sat back in her seat and looked out the window. She liked hugs. She'd heard Daddy tell Aunt Ruth he was going to ask somebody out on a date. She didn't like that. Daddy had Emma now.

They all did.

7

"WHAT ARE YOU doing up so late?"

Emma looked up from the cookbook she'd bought at the Methodist church table as Matt entered the kitchen and poured himself a glass of water. "I'm reading up on runzas," she confessed. "The Methodist ladies of Blindon contributed no less than four recipes for them."

"You're studying?" He looked amused and sat down across from her at the kitchen table. It was past ten, the children had been in bed for hours, and Emma had taken advantage of the quiet to make out a grocery list. Or at least, an attempt at one.

"I thought I'd better, since my pasta dish wasn't exactly a big hit last night."

"It wasn't that bad."

"It didn't have meat," she reminded him. "Everything you eat must have had hooves and mooed in a previous existence."

He took a long drink of water and leaned back in his chair. His face was coated with dirt and his clothes, a denim shirt and faded jeans, were spotted with dirt and perspiration. He had no right to be so handsome, she thought, looking at him. There was a lot to be said for the appeal of the Western man, though she'd never known any. Maybe that was it. She'd never met a rancher before.

"Why are you looking at me like that?"

Emma closed her cookbook. "I was thinking about laundry and how I have to get some wash done tomorrow."

"The washer and dryer are downstairs."

"I know. I saw them."

Matt studied her for a long moment. "Thanks for coming to town with us this afternoon. The girls really enjoyed having you there."

"It was fun," she said, and she meant it. "Everyone was very nice."

"I noticed." His lips twisted into a wry smile. "You could have had your pick of dates."

She shook her head. "I'm not interested."

He leaned forward, his elbows on the table. "You say that as if you meant it. Why?"

"That's a very long story." She hoped that would discourage him from asking anything else. How was she supposed to explain that she'd discovered her fiancé had preferred someone else fifteen minutes before the wedding was to begin?

"I have plenty of time."

Emma pushed the cookbook aside and stood. She

picked up her empty glass and placed it in the sink. "I was engaged once, and the man I was supposed to marry turned out to be in love with someone else."

Matt frowned, his dark gaze sympathetic. "Sorry. I shouldn't have pried into your business."

"That's okay," Emma said, hoping she sounded nonchalant. Hoping she sounded as if it had happened three years ago and not three days ago. Oh Lord, had it really been only three days since she'd stood in the church waiting to walk down the aisle on her father's arm?

"At least he told you the truth," Matt said.

"He didn't," she heard herself say. "He wasn't going to tell me at all, but when I found out... Well, I canceled the wedding and never saw him again. And I never want to."

"Good for you."

She managed to imitate a person smiling. "Yes, that's what I think, too."

There was silence for a moment while Matt stood. He drained the rest of his water and brought it over to the sink. "I'll make the coffee in the morning."

The change of subject was welcome. "What time do the girls get up?"

"They're running around by seven. Sometimes earlier." He seemed to hesitate. "Emma, thanks for taking the job. I think it's going to work out just fine." He leaned over to get the coffee out of the cabinet at the same time she moved to put the loaf of bread back in the cupboard. Her chest collided with his arm, leaving a tingling sensation that spread throughout her chest and sent a blush to her face.

"Sorry," she said.

"My fault," he said, and attempted to back away, but the wraparound counter had him trapped. "This kitchen wasn't designed for two people, I guess."

"No." Emma tossed the bread back on the counter and inched past the rancher. She had no business being attracted to him, but there was the matter of all that testosterone in one place, in one pair of jeans, in one very small area of the kitchen. She was only human. She had missed out on her wedding night.

"Good night," she said, moving toward the hall. A few more steps and she'd be alone with her raging hormones, thank goodness.

"Emma," Matt called. "We make our own breakfast around here, so don't worry about trying to cook in the morning."

She turned. "Don't the dogs like burned eggs?"

He smiled. "They're getting fat."

"I'm going to improve, you know." She walked over to the table and retrieved the cookbook.

"Yes, ma'am, I'm sure you are."

"Good night." Why was she reluctant to leave? Was it because Matt Thomson had turned out to have a sense of humor after all?

"Good night," he said, and turned away to fill the coffee carafe with water. Emma hurried down the hall and into her room. She shut the door and walked over to her closet to look at the "princess dress." It would serve as a reminder to beware of handsome men who had their own agenda. Matt Thomson needed a mother for his daughters. Ken had needed a fiancé so he would win the election.

And Emma didn't need anyone, she reminded herself. She was going to take a long, hot bath and read her cookbook. She might not know anything about men, but she was committed to the kitchen.

For now.

MACKIE TURNED OUT to be good company. Cheerful and loving, she stayed close to Emma while she negotiated her way through the aisles of groceries in the Blindon Market. Emma had instructions to charge the food to the Triple Creek account, which turned out to be a good thing, since she bought so much of it. She managed to get the bags of groceries and the three-year-old into the wide station wagon without too much of a struggle, then found the kindergarten after taking two wrong turns. Which brought her back to where she started, in front of Stu's in the middle of Blindon.

Mackie giggled. Melissa, waiting outside, looked relieved, and the three of them returned to the ranch for lunch just as Matt crossed the driveway to his truck. He stopped when Emma parked the station wagon near the back door. "Groceries?"

"Groceries and girls," Emma said. "All home safe and sound and I was only lost once."

He smiled in that attractive way of his. "How could you get lost in Blindon?"

She stepped out of the car and shrugged. "I have no sense of direction." The girls tumbled out of the car to greet their father, leaving Emma with a clear path to the bags of groceries piled on the car floor.

"I'll help you with those." He came around and grabbed several paper bags while Emma piled two in her arms and headed for the back door.

"Mackie, hold the door," her father ordered. "Mel, you find a light bag and bring it in."

"Were you waiting for lunch?" she asked, following him into the kitchen. "Mackie said she likes cheese sandwiches, so I thought I'd toast—"

"I already ate, thanks." He piled bags on the kitchen table and went out for the rest of them while she began to search through the bags to find the cheese she'd bought for lunch. He returned with another armload, which he dumped on the table.

"There, that's all of it." He turned to Emma. "Looks like you plan to be cooking for a while."

"I'm going to try."

He nodded. "I appreciate that."

"You do?"

"Yeah." Mackie reached up to him for a hug, so he picked her up. She promptly wrapped her arms around his neck and kissed his cheek.

"You're so good with her," Emma murmured, not bothering to hide her surprise.

"Why wouldn't I be?" He frowned a little. "I'm her father."

"I didn't mean that to be insulting," she said, glad she could look away from him and search the grocery bag in front of her. "My own father wasn't very affectionate. I guess I meant that I envy your daughters."

Which, of course, came out all wrong. She blushed. Would he think she wanted to wrap her arms around his neck, too? "I—I mean," she stammered, "I just—"

The phone rang, and she returned to the groceries while Matt lifted the receiver.

"Hey, Steph," he said. "Yeah, everything's fine. How are you doin'?"

"Auntie Steph!" Mackie hollered and ran to her father's knees. "Can I talk?"

"In a minute, honey," her father said, while Emma shamelessly eavesdropped. "Ruth called you? Well, yeah, it's going fine. You don't have to worry." Silence. "I can't get away until Thanksgiving. You know that."

Another silence while he listened to his sister. "You're welcome to come down anytime. What's Clay up to these days?"

Clay must be Stephanie's husband, Emma realized. And Stephanie was worried about the children's new housekeeper and wanted them to visit.

"Yeah, I know," Matt murmured. "She worries a lot about nothing, but you know how she is."

Ruth. She quietly lifted a bag of white rice from the next brown paper bag and set it on the table.

"Here, talk to Mackie. No, come on up whenever you can. We'll talk about Thanksgiving when it gets a little closer, I promise." He handed the receiver to his daughter and both he and Emma listened to Mackie describe her ballet slippers and her new clothes until she finally said goodbye and handed her father the receiver to replace on its hook.

"My sister," Matt said. "She likes to plan holidays years in advance. She's already trying to figure out Thanksgiving."

By Thanksgiving Emma would be back in Chicago. The election would be over and her father would be immersed in another round of business decisions and political strategies and she would be free to…do what? Find an apartment and get a life? It was about time. Emma forced herself back to the conversation. "Your sister must love her nieces very much."

Matt frowned. "Yes." He lifted Mackie in his arms and gave her a hug. "We all do."

HER DAYS FELL into a pattern quickly, faster than Emma would have predicted. She spent her mornings getting the girls ready for school, driving them where they needed to go, doing errands in town, planning the meals, and studying cookbooks for easy recipes. In the afternoon she did laundry, tucked Mackie into her bed for a nap, played with Melissa on the porch and ran the vacuum cleaner only if the carpet looked messy. The television in the living room wasn't hooked to an antenna—Matt said the darn thing blew off in a windstorm last month and he hadn't had time to fix it—and the children didn't appear to care. Emma decided she didn't, either. She heard the local news on the car radio when she drove the children back and forth and that was enough.

The house was quiet, including the phone. Ranch business was handled in the main bunkhouse; pickup trucks didn't stop at the main house but continued down the road to the buildings to the west.

Sometimes she took the girls for a walk. They would look at the horses in the corral or try to find the kittens that were no longer small enough to be called kittens. The cowboys would wave and grin, then go back to work. The wind blew incessantly, but she loved looking at the distant horizon, especially at sunset.

Matt joined them for dinner every night promptly at six, but often he left again to do more chores. She wondered if the rancher really had that much work or if he was in the bunkhouse watching television with the other men.

Ruth came by twice. Once to tell her that she would take the girls to church and that she would supply Sunday's dinner, since that was "the help's day off."

Emma had thanked her, slept late on Sunday morning, then took the station wagon and drove west for hours, until it was time to turn around and come back to the ranch. Freedom, isolation and a car full of gas were wonderful things.

It was Tuesday before Matt asked her a direct question.

"Have you ever been to a sale barn?"

"What?" The word *sale* caught her attention.

"A sale barn. I go once or twice a week."

"Why?" She found the cheese, thank goodness. Melissa opened the refrigerator and grabbed a gallon of milk, which Emma rescued before it fell on the floor.

"That's my business." His voice was patient, but she felt his gaze on her as she walked around the counter and took two plastic cups from the cupboard. "I sell cattle. I buy cattle."

"Right." She poured the milk into the two glasses. "Ladies, if you want a drink you will have to sit at the table." Mackie scrambled out of her father's arms and Mel hurried to join her at the table.

"It can be interesting."

"The sale barn?"

"Yes. They're a big part of ranch life. There are ten of them within a hundred mile radius."

She had no idea what he was talking about, but she liked the fact that he was talking to her. That in itself was something to enjoy. "Is that where you're headed?"

"Yes." He hesitated. "I'll see if Ruth can watch the kids this afternoon. You might as well see what we do with cattle." With that he left the kitchen and Emma heard the screen door slam shut.

"You're lucky," Melissa said, her eyes wide as Emma placed the milk in front of her.

"I am?"

"Yep. If you're real good and sit still and don't say anything, Daddy will buy you a candy bar for the ride home."

She had to laugh. "Really?"

"Yep. Any kind you want."

"Then I'll have to make sure I behave myself."

Though how she was supposed to behave in a sale barn, she had no idea.

"Foolish," Ruth grumbled. "Taking that woman to a cattle auction in the middle of the week."

"Lots of women go."

"Wives," his aunt said. "They're ranchers' wives and they're helping out the men. They're not pretty housekeepers from the city."

Matt didn't care. "I thought she'd enjoy seeing an auction. It's always quite a show."

"If you wanted company, one of the boys could have gone with you."

Jasper, Pete, Bobby or Chet wouldn't smell like roses. They didn't have green eyes and silky chestnut hair and they didn't look so good in their jeans the way Emma did. Damn it, what was wrong with wanting a little female companionship? Besides the females in his life that were under the age of eight, that is. "Come on, Ruth. Just come sit in the living room while Mackie sleeps and Melissa does whatever she does in the afternoon."

"And is your housekeeper fixing dinner?"

"She bought enough food to last till Halloween," Matt said. "I suppose there's something in there for dinner tonight."

"And what if you're late?"

Matt put his hands on his hips and stared down at

his aunt. Lord knows he loved the woman, but she could try anyone's patience. "Aunt Ruth, why don't you like Emma?"

Ruth fumbled in the pocket of her housedress for a tissue. She wiped her eyes and sniffed. "I don't want to see you hurt again, Matthew. These city women just can't be trusted. She could have a husband somewhere, for all we know. Or she could be a criminal. Or a...fallen woman."

"I don't think she's any of those things, Ruth." At least, he hoped not. Especially the part about having a husband somewhere. "She told me she was supposed to get married, but she ended up calling it off."

"Did she say why?"

"No," he fibbed, unwilling to discuss Emma's personal life. Ruth would think nothing of pursuing the conversation with Emma the first chance she got. "All that matters is that we have some help around here."

"Stephanie's going to have a fit. Has she called?"

"Twice, but I let the machine pick it up this last time. I'll call her back tonight and tell her how we're doing." He gazed down at his aunt. Either she was going to get with the program or not. "How are we doing?"

Ruth sighed. "Let me get my yarn. I'm working on

an afghan for Bobby's bed. He wore out that old one, you know."

Matt knew. Ruth's afghans were prized possessions and treated with tenderness by otherwise rowdy men. The elderly woman was a devoted friend and a formidable opponent. He wished she'd ease up on Emma. "Thanks."

Ruth disappeared into her bedroom and returned with a plastic sack stuffed with blue yarn. "Just do me a favor, Matthew."

"Anything, Ruth." He took the bag while she grabbed her cane.

"Just tell me you're not going to fall in love with her."

"I'm not," he promised. He had no intention of falling in love again, but he sure wouldn't mind a little female companionship.

"Good," she declared, thumping her cane toward the door. "We could do without the complications."

Matt hid his sigh. He would look forward to a few complications if that meant having a warm and willing woman in his bed at night.

"DON'T MOVE THIS TIME."

He noticed she was careful to stare straight ahead and keep her hands in her lap. "Okay," she whispered through barely parted lips.

Matt would have laughed, but because ten

minutes ago he'd almost bought a sow and ten little pigs when Emma scratched her nose, he'd prefer the woman to hold still. He had nothing against hogs. They brought in good money and he appreciated bacon as much as the next man, but he sure didn't need any more hogs right before winter. The auctioneer banged his gavel and yelled, "Sold!"

Emma turned to Matt. "It's okay if I breathe now?"

"Sure. Go ahead."

She leaned back in the metal seat and looked down into the sawdust-covered arena. "What are they doing?"

He took a sip of his coffee and so did Emma. "Bringing in cattle. That's what we came for."

"It is? I mean, don't you have enough already?"

"Not exactly. I buy and sell according to the market and the season and the stock on the ranch. Right now I'm looking for some decent bull stock. And I'll be selling stock I don't want to feed throughout the winter."

"How can you tell when anyone is bidding?"

"The auctioneer knows. Some people are obvious, while others just wink or tap their program." He couldn't help chuckling at the expression on her face. "Like you almost bought hogs."

She grimaced. "That would have taken care of a month's salary."

"At least, and you would have had to take care of them, too," he teased, wondering why such a pretty woman was all alone in the world. "Who are you, Emma? And why are you alone?"

She turned away from him and pretended to watch the cattle being herded into the small enclosure in front of the auctioneer's podium. "Why did you bring me here today?"

"I thought you'd enjoy it." And I didn't want to be alone.

"I am."

She took another sip of her coffee and placed the foam cup at her feet and finally answered his question. "I'm here because I needed a job. Can we leave it at that?"

"Yes, ma'am, if that's what you want."

She glanced at him, those green eyes of hers full of sadness. "Yes, that's exactly what I want."

Matt nodded. "Well, I *don't* want those Angus heifers, so you sit real still while the bidding is going on."

"Don't worry about me," Emma said. "You won't even know I'm here."

As if that was possible.

EMMA DIDN'T KNOW what was wrong with heating up the frozen chicken potpies. They'd looked cute in the grocery freezer section. Little individual pies in little boxes would certainly appeal to the children. But no, Ruth Tuttle baked a meat loaf and meat loaf they would have. Ruth hadn't bothered taking the chicken pies from the freezer.

Emma ate a dry slice of meat and figured she'd heat up those chicken pies another night. The elderly woman had gone to a lot of trouble to make dinner while Emma had been relaxing in a sale barn fifty miles north of town. Not relaxing, exactly. Sitting that close to Matt Thomson could not be called relaxing, not at all. He was all male, and the body that was encased in the brown plaid shirt and blue jeans was long, lean and muscular.

Melissa wiggled on her chair. "Did Daddy buy you a candy bar, Emma?"

"No, he didn't." She winked at the child. "I guess I didn't sit still. I'll be better next time."

Ruth snorted. "Next time? You planning on being a rancher?"

Emma ignored her and turned to Martha. "How was school today?"

"Jennifer liked my new outfit," the little girl said. "Want to see my papers? We made up a story about a wagon train."

"I'd love to read it," she assured her. "What else did you do today?"

Martha brightened. "We read a new story."

"Red like cherries?" Melissa asked.

"No," her sister sighed. "Read like read a book. You know, read."

"Oh." Melissa stabbed a chunk of meat loaf. "Not red like ketchup."

Martha turned back to Emma. "My tooth is loose."

"Congratulations." She hoped that was the right thing to say, but Martha gave her a strange look.

"Don't you want to know which one?"

"Which one?"

"The bottom one. Maybe it will fall out tonight and I'll put it under my pillow." Martha looked at her father. "You know, Daddy, the Tooth Fairy can come, right?"

"Oh, sure." Matt reached for the ketchup and covered his slice of meat loaf with it. "The Tooth Fairy."

"It's very loose," Martha said. "Wanna see?"

"Not here," Emma reminded her. "Your father will look at it later."

"And you, too?"

"Of course." She turned to Mackie and cut her meat. Ruth had made rice and corn. "Thank you again for making dinner."

"You're welcome. No telling how late you were going to be. If Matt had bought any stock, you'd get home late. These ranchers can get carried away and lose track of time." She turned to Martha. "Eat a piece of bread. Maybe that'll do it."

"Do what?"

"Take her tooth out." The old woman pushed the platter of meat loaf toward Emma. "Have some more. You city women are all too thin."

She took a small piece so she wouldn't hurt Ruth's feelings.

"You bought a lot of groceries," the woman said. "You planning some fancy meals?"

"Not really. I was just looking through the cookbooks and I thought I'd try a few, um, new recipes." She looked over to Matt. "Right, Matt? Didn't you say you wanted something different for a change?"

"That's right," he said, helping himself to another helping of rice. "I surely did."

"Always thought food was food," Ruth grumbled. "Give me plain, home-cooked meals any day."

"There's nothing wrong with something new once in a while," Emma said. "I'm going to experiment with runzas tomorrow."

Ruth rolled her eyes to the ceiling. "Lord help us."

"Don't worry," Emma said sweetly. "I'm not going to throw any at you, Ruth."

Matt chuckled. "If she gets any crankier you might have to."

Ruth surprised Emma by smiling. "Now, Matthew, I always thought I was an easy woman to get along with."

He shook his head. "If you'll pass me some more

meat loaf I promise to change the subject and talk about the weather or the price of corn."

Melissa spilled her milk, Emma wiped up the mess, Martha wiggled her tooth for everyone to see, and Ruth slid her chair back away from the table when it came time to clear the dishes.

In other words, Emma thought, it was another typical evening at the Thomson house. And amazingly, she was part of it. At least for the time being.

8

"YOU'RE GOING TO have to help me with this." Matt reached into his pocket and pulled out a handful of change. "How much is a tooth worth these days?"

Emma looked up from the stack of cookbooks. She had a pile of paper in front of her and she looked like she'd spent the evening taking notes on food. He didn't know why she was so determined to cook something different. He didn't mind hamburgers and there was enough steak in the freezer to fry until next May. "I wouldn't have any idea. How much change do you have?"

He sifted through the coins. "Fifty, seventy-five, eighty-five, ninety...two."

"Ninety-two cents should be enough."

Matt looked at the clock above the stove. It was after nine and the house had been quiet for an hour. "Do you think they're asleep?"

She listened for a second. "It sounds very quiet up there."

"Did they give you any trouble about going to bed?"

"No. I think they were all tired and Mackie was so excited about going to school tomorrow that she wore herself out by seven-thirty."

"She likes school."

Emma smiled. "Yes. She can't wait for the time when she can go to school every day like her big sisters."

"You're very good with them." The girls needed a mother. That much was obvious by the way they adored Emma and sought her attention like three little ducklings quacking after the mother duck. He wondered if they'd been that way at his sister's house in Omaha—or was it Emma who was special? He wished he knew, wished he knew if he was making the right decisions, but all he was sure of right now was that the Tooth Fairy had better make a visit to Martha or there would be hell to pay tomorrow morning.

She smiled. "Do you really think so? I haven't been around children very much. I was an only child."

He wondered if she realized she'd just revealed some personal information. "Who was the Tooth Fairy in your house, your mother or your father?"

"I have no idea. I lived in boarding schools where they didn't hold with such nonsense."

"Nonsense," he repeated, looking down at the

coins in his palm. "Maybe it is, but it makes the children happy."

"I didn't mean that it was nonsense," she said quickly, looking worried when he met her gaze across the room. "Only that my teachers thought anything like that was ridiculous and not to be encouraged."

"Doesn't sound like much of a childhood."

"It had its ups and downs." She closed the cookbook and stood. "How do we act like the Tooth Fairy? You'll have to show me."

"Come on. You have to be very quiet so we don't wake them."

"What do we do if she wakes up?"

"I pretend I was checking her before I went to bed and then hope that she doesn't remember in the morning."

"That sounds like a good plan," she said, following him into the hall and up the staircase. "Have you done this a lot?"

"Nope." He hadn't taken a woman upstairs since Patty died, either. There had been other housekeepers, but none that made him feel as if he were walking on eggs whenever she was around him. He didn't like feeling so unsettled.

"What's the matter?"

He glanced toward her as he turned on the small night-light in the hall. "Nothing. Why?"

"You were frowning. And not looking like a Tooth Fairy at all," she whispered.

"Come on." He carefully opened the door to Martha and Melissa's room. Emma hung back.

"What am I supposed to do?" Her whisper swept the back of his neck.

"Help me find the tooth," Matt explained, keeping his voice quiet. "Your hands are smaller than mine." They tiptoed across the room, past Melissa's bed. The child was snuggled under her sheet, her hair a jumbled dark mass of curls on the white pillow. Martha lay sprawled on top of her covers, her arms spread wide apart and her little mouth open. She looked like someone who had had a long day and had collapsed the second she hit the mattress. He lifted the edge of the pillow and motioned for Emma to slide her hand underneath and find the tooth.

She gave him a questioning look, but managed to feel around and pull out a folded piece of paper. Matt handed her the money and watched as she carefully slid the change under the pillow without disturbing Martha's head more than a fraction of an inch.

He nodded and they left the room together. Matt shut the door behind them and Emma paused. "Here," she said, handing him the wad of paper. "Do you keep these?"

"I don't know. I guess so."

He unfolded the paper and captured the little tooth as it tumbled toward his palm. "Dear Tooth Fairy," he read aloud. "Thanks for coming to my house. Love, Martha."

"Cute."

"She likes to write letters." He folded the paper and tucked it in his shirt pocket.

"Does the Tooth Fairy write back?"

Matt considered that for a second. "No. Too risky."

"I guess you're right. Well, I'd better go to bed," Emma said. "Good night." She hesitated. "Thanks again for taking me to the cattle sale. I had a good time, even though I did almost make you buy a hog."

He chuckled. "We could have made room." She was close, close enough to touch if he had the courage. Those slanted green eyes with their dark lashes and teasing expression gazed up at him and turned his heart upside down. He held the fleeting image of her small hand sliding along the sheet as Emma moved toward the stairs.

"I'd better go, before Martha wakes up and hears the Tooth Fairy talking in the hall. Good—"

"What about the Easter Bunny?" he had to ask, unwilling to let her leave him alone in the hall. They stood very close together; he wondered how that happened. "Were you given baskets filled with jelly beans and chocolate when you were a child?"

"Yes. My father always presented me with a Godiva rabbit. With a yellow satin bow around its neck."

"And what about Santa Claus?"

She shook her head, and his came lower. Her lips were full and pink, her cheekbones shadowed in the dim light. "I always hoped he was real, but my governess told me differently."

"And now?" He touched her lips with his in the barest caress, so light he wondered if he'd touched her at all. There was the scent of roses from her hair, a fleeting warmth from her skin, a faint trace of passion in the kiss. Matt retreated slightly, inches away from her mouth, as he braced himself with one arm against the wall.

"Now I don't believe in fairy tales." There was an ironic twist to her mouth that surprised him. "If I ever did."

"Your fiancé." The man who'd left her for another woman had to be an idiot.

She gazed up at him. "It's easier not to believe in anything."

"Except yourself," he reminded her. "And this." With that he leaned closer and tasted those lips again. He didn't touch her, deliberately kept his hand at his side and the other on the wall while he urged her lips apart and tasted her mouth. She was hot and sweet, quick to passion and equally quick to end the embrace.

"No" was all she said before she turned and hurried down the stairs. Matt felt like a fool. He had no business kissing the housekeeper. No business kissing Emma Gray, a woman who had shown him only the mildest sort of friendship for the past eleven days.

Matt banged his hand against the wall. He didn't know what had gotten into him, but whatever it was it had to stop. From now on, he would keep his distance. Emma Gray would never be interested in a widowed rancher, never be interested in living in the middle of nowhere with someone else's children. And there was no reason why she should be.

He had to put that vision out of his mind. She was temporary. And then he would find someone else to take her place. Or he would marry.

And he would forget all about Emma Gray and her broken heart.

SHE WOULD LEAVE. Emma assumed that with kisses came the automatic cancellation of her agreement with Matt Thomson. She could not stay two months. She could not even stay the two weeks trial period upon which they'd both agreed. She could not stay and hope for him to kiss her again, all the time knowing that she was foolish to want him to. Ten—no, eleven—days ago she had been ready and willing to marry someone else. Oh, she'd known there was passion lacking there. It hadn't been at all like the couples in the movies, but she knew that life was different. Life was companionship and compromise, friendship and shared interests. As long as she had shared Ken's interests, she would have had a happy marriage.

Or so she'd thought. She snuggled in her bed and closed her eyes, willing herself to banish the memory of that scene in the church. What a fool she'd been not to see. What a fool she'd been to believe Ken's sweet words of love, and not question his insistence of waiting until their wedding night to make love to each other.

She was no longer a fool, no longer willing to believe what she was told. No, there wasn't an Easter Bunny, or a Tooth Fairy or a Santa Claus. If there was a "happily ever after" she sure hadn't found it yet.

And here, in just a short period of time, she'd realized she adored children. She'd let their father kiss her and, to her dismay, she'd kissed him back. And enjoyed it.

And wanted more.

It was best she leave. She tossed the covers aside and padded across the room to her purse where she counted her money. She had seventy-eight dollars and Matt's check for a week's pay. Surely she could catch a bus to the nearest town, North Platte she supposed, and then wire Paula for money. Not for the first time, she cursed herself for not having a bank account separate from her father. She'd thought that arrangement was fine until she turned thirty and could access her trust fund. Foolish, but then again, she hadn't exactly been a Mensa candidate for the past year or so. She'd been a foolish woman who'd thought she was in love and trusted the men in her life to make her decisions for her.

Emma put her money away and returned to her bed. From now on she would make her own decisions. Just let anyone try to tell her differently.

IT WAS ONE thing to decide to leave. It was another thing to find someone to inform. Matt wasn't around on Wednesday morning. The only trace of his existence was an empty cup in the sink and half a pot of hot coffee in the carafe. She drove Melissa and Martha to meet the school bus at the end of the road, then gave Mackie a bath and readied her for play school.

She was getting good at this, Emma realized, although she had yet to do much real housecleaning and the cooking had elevated to a "edible but barely" status. The Thomsons had gamely chewed their way through any number of experiments. She would vacuum again before she left, and change the sheets on the beds and maybe even wash the kitchen floor. A rancher's housekeeper could make an entire career out of trying to keep the floor clean.

"Dance today?" Mackie held up the ballet slippers.

"After the girls come home from school," Emma promised, realizing that her departure would have to be postponed. A promise was a promise, after all. But tomorrow she would go. Right after she froze some casseroles so Matt wouldn't have to worry about supper for the rest of the week.

It was the least she could do.

She didn't leave on Thursday, either, because Mackie had a little cold which on Friday turned into an earache which required an antibiotic. Saturday afternoon, when she came back to the ranch after taking the child to the local physician, her only concern was dealing with a feverish child. Spooning thick pink medicine into a three-year-old turned out to be something Emma needed Matt's help with. He'd been avoiding her—except for supper time the children wouldn't have known they had a father. And even then he'd spoken so infrequently she wondered if she remembered the sound of his voice.

She took Melissa outside with her, leaving Martha to amuse Mackie for a few minutes until their father could be found. One of the ranch hands guessed he might be in the tractor shed, and sure enough, that was where she found him. The huge doors were wide open, allowing the warm breeze access to the shed. Matt was tinkering with the engine of the tractor and cursing softly under his breath.

She didn't bother with hellos.

"Mackie has an ear infection," she informed Matt. "The doctor said it's pretty common at this age, but she has medicine to take and she won't take it."

Melissa left Emma's side and ran to her father. "It's pink, like bubble gum!"

Matt tousled the child's hair and frowned. "She's always been bad at taking medicine."

"If you have any tips on how to get her to swallow it, I would certainly appreciate hearing them. That is, if you have the time," she couldn't help adding. She stood in the doorway, unwilling to step closer to him. He'd kissed her days ago; he'd avoided her ever since. That didn't do much for a woman's ego, even if that woman had shoved her few possessions into a plastic garbage bag twice since the last time they'd been alone and sworn to herself that she would leave as soon as she could figure out how.

"No problem," he said, giving her a sharp look before he hung the wrench on the wall. "All you had to do was ask."

"You haven't been around to ask."

"I'm sorry." His voice was mild. "I thought you'd rather have it that way."

She didn't know how to answer, so she walked beside him back to the house. Melissa kept up a constant stream of chatter about school, how big the kittens were growing, the cherry-flavored Jell-O she'd helped make and how she'd even put little marshmallows on top so Mackie would be happy and not cry about how her ear hurt.

"That sounds real good," Matt said to everything Melissa said. Emma wondered if Melissa told her father that Emma had burned all of his plaid shirts and set fire to the outhouse, he would still continue to reply in the same distracted manner.

When they arrived back at the house, he turned out to be good at giving medicine, though. She had to give him credit when he winked at Martha, put Mackie on his knee, whispered in her ear, and gave her a spoonful of medicine. She made a face, but she swallowed the pink liquid without protest. Emma took Mackie from Matt and carried her up to bed, where she snuggled with her teddy bears and closed her eyes in contentment.

Emma hurried downstairs before Matt could escape outside once again. He sat alone at the table, a cup of coffee in front of him. "How did you do that?"

"Bribery. A chocolate shake for every day she has to take the medicine."

"I should have known. I'll have to remember that one." Emma emptied the coffeepot into her mug and pulled up a chair near Matthew. Probably too close, but what the heck. She was leaving soon and there was no harm in sitting beside him in the kitchen. "Unless it only works for fathers."

"Sometimes bribery is the only option," Matt said ruefully, taking a sip of his coffee. He leaned back in his chair and gave her a searching look. "What's up, Emma? You look ready to bust."

"Where are the girls?"

"Off to Ruth's for a while."

Then she could talk without being overheard or interrupted. "I've been here two weeks."

"And?"

"That was the trial period, remember?"

"I remember."

"And I don't think it has worked out."

He stared at her, his expression unreadable. After long moments of silence he finally spoke. "And you're leaving?"

"I think that's what I should do, yes."

"Because of what happened the other night."

This time she hesitated. She didn't want to talk about that, or think about that, or deal with that. "I think I should get on with my life. It's about time."

"What the heck does that mean?"

"It means, I think I should leave."

"Yeah, well," he muttered. He rose and dumped the rest of his coffee into the sink and set the mug on the counter. "You sure have a lot of 'shoulds.'" He turned to look down at her as she stood. "I promised I wouldn't touch you again."

"That isn't—"

He reached out and cupped her chin with his hand. His fingers were rough against her skin. "Yes, it is. That's what it's all about, lady. You've had your fur up since that night upstairs."

"I think I should—"

"*Should* again. What do you want to do, Emma?" Those dark eyes stared into hers, daring her to answer with the truth, and he tilted her chin so her lips were closer to his.

"I want to leave," she heard herself reply, but she spoke to his mouth, unwilling to look away.

"Then you're certainly free to go," he said, touching his lips to hers. It wasn't the gentle exploration of last week, but an intense heat that made her step closer to him, into the kiss and against that wide, warm, solid chest. His arms wrapped around her and held her to him as if she were going to disappear if he didn't. She wanted to kiss him forever. Passion rose, hot and demanding, between them until she thought she would fall into a heap on the floor and bring him down with her.

He lifted his mouth from hers. "I shouldn't have done that, but I wanted to."

"Yes, so did I," she admitted, her voice a whisper.

She was surprised she could talk, especially since her body seemed to be humming an unfamiliar yet not unpleasant song.

"Is that why you're leaving, Emma?" He released her and took a step backward. "Because we're... attracted to each other?"

"Partly." If she could have lied she would have. "I have commitments, family, things to settle back home."

"Why don't I believe you?"

"You should."

"*Should* again." His lips turned down. "Tell me what you want, sweetheart."

She wanted to be called sweetheart and kissed like that again. When he kissed her she forgot about Ken and his lover. She forgot her father's anger and disappointment, her wounded pride and the wedding that—thankfully—never took place and the marriage that would have been a sham.

"I want to leave," she managed to say and saw the light leave his eyes. "As soon as Mackie is better."

He held up his hands, palms toward her, as if to say he had given up. "Don't do me any favors. You're free to leave, of course. Anytime you wish. You can catch a ride to town with Ruth when she goes to church tomorrow. There's a bus to North Platte in the afternoon."

He sounded almost glad to get rid of her. "I can wait," she began, but Matt shook his head.

"You can leave tomorrow. The sooner the better." He reached for his hat and slammed it on his head. "I just hope you know what you're doing."

She watched him leave the kitchen and hoped she knew what she was doing, too. She would go back to Chicago now. Her father couldn't possibly still be angry after two weeks. The dust would have settled; the election would be in high gear. Surely by now the press would have found something else to write about.

Surely she could continue on with her life as if Emma Gray had never existed.

9

"THEY WERE KISSING," Martha announced to Melissa and Ruth. The three of them were seated around Aunt Ruth's tiny little kitchen table and were about to play a game. "I saw them."

Ruth frowned at her. "You shouldn't be telling stories, young lady." She wiggled in the chair and then winced, as if her leg hurt her again. Ruth's leg hurt a lot, Daddy said. That's why she couldn't take care of them any more and they had to get baby-sitters.

"I'm not telling stories. I really saw them. Daddy likes Emma and Emma likes Daddy." Martha plopped the deck of cards on the table and shoved them toward Aunt Ruth, who could shuffle without dropping the cards on the floor. "Neat, huh?"

Aunt Ruth just stared at her. "Where were they kissing?"

"On the lips." She giggled and so did Melissa.

"No, Martha. Where in the house did you see this?"

"In the kitchen. I went back to ask Emma if she

wanted to play Go Fish with us but she was kissing Daddy so I didn't ask her."

"Hmmmph." She took the cards, divided the deck in half and shuffled the way Martha tried to copy and couldn't. "I'd have to see it to believe it, young lady. Emma isn't the type to fall for a rancher with cow manure on his boots and hay in his hair."

"Daddy scrapes his boots," Melissa insisted. "We all hafta before we can come in the house. Are we gonna play Go Fish or Kings in the Corner?"

"Go Fish," Melissa said.

"Go Fish has my vote." Ruth dealt the cards. "Martha, go get me my medicine, will you? It's in my bedroom by my bed."

"Sure." Martha scrambled off the chair. She loved Aunt Ruth's little house. It was like a dollhouse, only bigger, with no stairs and wallpaper covered with pink and red roses. Aunt Ruth had baskets of yarn, pretty bowls filled with hard candy, boxes of jigsaw puzzles and, best of all, a television that worked. Martha found the medicine and ran back to the kitchen to give it to her aunt. "Is your leg hurting, Auntie?"

"Yep." Ruth swallowed her pills with the rest of her tea. "This old hip is giving me fits today."

"I'm sorry," Martha said, starting to get worried. "Want to get on the couch and watch TV while we play?"

Aunt Ruth sighed, then winced as she struggled to her feet and leaned on her cane. "I think that's a real good idea, honey. Maybe if I lie down I can get these old bones to stop aching."

"Kissing," Melissa repeated, looking disappointed that she hadn't seen it. Martha scooped up her cards and Aunt Ruth's, while Melissa grabbed hers and held them close to her chest. "Kissing?"

"Yep. Just like on TV."

"Oh, heavens," Aunt Ruth muttered. "Don't go telling your dad that I let you watch 'Days of Our Lives.' I'll never hear the end of it." She stopped and leaned in the doorway to rest.

Martha followed her. "What's wrong with kissing? Daddy can marry Emma and we'll have a mommy." Having a mom like all of the other girls would be the best thing in the whole world. She didn't like telling people that her mom died a long time ago. "I want a mom like everyone else has."

Aunt Ruth groaned. "Emma isn't like everyone else. The woman doesn't even know how to cook."

Melissa giggled. "Daddy likes the way Emma cooks. When she burns stuff he doesn't get mad and he gives it to the dogs."

"No one cooks on 'Days of Our Lives,'" Martha said, waiting for Aunt Ruth to move to the living room and sit on the couch. It was the best couch, all squishy and soft, and afghans folded on top of the cushions so anyone who wanted to could snuggle inside a blanket.

"Better go find your Dad, girls," Ruth gasped, tilting over a chair. "I'm goin' down."

THE MINUTE MATT carried Ruth into the house, Emma knew she was going to stay. Tomorrow's bus to North Platte would leave without her, and that was fine. Surprisingly fine.

"Put her on the couch," Emma suggested. "She'll be comfortable there, and that way we can keep an eye on her."

Matt gave her a questioning look. "We? I thought you were leaving."

She didn't answer him. She was too busy trying to find the closet where the clean linens were stored.

Later, when Ruth was settled on the couch, Emma used her best "nurse" voice and approached the woman. "Do you want some tea, Ruth? Or a cold drink?"

"No, Emma, I'm fine. I'll be out of your way as soon as I can." Ruth groaned and shifted onto her side. "These spells don't last too long, thank the good Lord."

"Well, if I can get you anything..." Emma hesitated, unsure if Ruth was able to be left alone. Not that the living room was that far away, but still, Ruth was old and in pain. She'd sent the girls upstairs for a little while, just until she could see that Ruth was settled. Matt was up on the roof trying to fix the television antenna so Ruth would have something to watch while she was laid up.

"You just go do whatever it is you have to do. Matt said your two weeks are up and you're catching a bus tomorrow. Is that right?"

Emma lifted her chin and met Ruth's gaze. "No, that's not right. I'm not about to leave now, not when you can't even get off the couch. Who would take care of the girls?"

"I suspect we'd manage, just the way we've done before."

Emma dropped into a chair. She hadn't sat in the living room very often, but now was as good a time as any to confront Matt's aunt. "You don't like me. Why not?"

"City folk have no business being out here."

"Aren't you being a little unfair? I was hired to take care of the children, not run a ranch."

"You know exactly what I mean, missy. Unfair is what Matthew's wife did to him, and she was a city girl, too. You'd think the boy had learned his lesson but instead he brings home another skinny woman with long fingernails and fancy hair who has no idea how to run a house or cook a decent meal for hardworking men." Ruth closed her eyes and leaned back on her pillow. The pillow that Emma had supplied and plumped for her. "It just breaks my heart to see it happening all over again."

"To see what happening all over again?"

Ruth opened her eyes and glared at her. "Matt needs to marry again. He and I have talked about a few women—*local* women—who would make good ranch wives. You weren't one of them."

Okay, Emma thought, her feelings shouldn't be hurt, but they were. "I'm not exactly shopping for a husband, Ruth."

"Martha saw you kissing her father today. You might want to think about what those children are thinking."

"What do you mean?"

"I mean," Ruth said, her voice rising, "that those little girls think that you're going to be their new mother. And heaven only knows what Matthew thinks."

Matt's voice blasted loud and clear from the front porch. "Matt thinks you should mind your own business and turn on the television," he said. "Let me know if channel twelve is coming in clear or not."

Emma felt her face grow hot and Ruth swallowed hard. They looked away from each other. Then Emma got up and turned on the television.

"Good," Ruth declared, as a football game came into focus. "We can watch Notre Dame get stomped until the Nebraska game starts. I just love college football, don't you?''

HE DIDN'T KNOW what he was going to do. Emma wanted to leave, Ruth was on the living room couch watching football and giving orders, Mackie was still feverish, and there were calves to round up and sell while the price of beef was still good enough to make some kind of profit to start paying for the new tractor that had been delivered last Friday.

Matt wondered where he'd gone wrong. He'd thought he was doing the right thing when he brought home a housekeeper. He'd thought he would relieve Ruth and circumvent Stephanie. Instead, he'd caused one heck of a commotion.

He went into the kitchen, took a bottle of whiskey from the top shelf of a kitchen cabinet, and poured himself a small glass. It went down real smooth, real warm. Oh, he knew he shouldn't have kissed her. No, he darn well should have. Didn't know how he couldn't have kissed her, with her standing there looking up at him like that and talking about leaving.

It was the talk about leaving that had pushed him over the edge of reason and into kissing that woman right in the middle of the day, right in the middle of the kitchen where anyone could see.

Where Martha had seen.

He was attracted to Emma. Lord knows he was attracted to Emma, but after almost four years of celibacy he couldn't be counted on to make realistic decisions. Maybe Ruth was right. Emma wasn't the ideal ranch wife, but he wasn't looking to fill a job position. He wanted a wife, a partner, a lover. He wanted a warm body beside his at night. He wanted to hear a woman complain about his cold feet. He wanted to feel that woman—his woman—touch him in the dark hours before sleep. He didn't care about cooking or cleaning or if she knew a heifer from a steer, as long as she loved him.

And there was the problem, Matt decided. Love. He wasn't in love with anyone. If he had a choice, he'd pick Alice or Gerta. Or some pleasant local woman he hadn't even met yet. He'd never pick a beautiful stranger he'd met in Gold's, a woman who insisted his rowdy daughters should own ballet shoes and who thought round steak should actually be round.

Matt finished his whiskey and then stood up to grab his hat. There were five females in his house right now, five females who would want to talk to him and give him an opinion on something. Matt sat back down and poured himself another shot of whiskey. He would deal with them all later, but for now he was going to enjoy the peace and quiet.

Besides, looking at Emma made him ache. He didn't think that had anything to do with being in love, though. That was an entirely different subject altogether.

PAULA DIDN'T UNDERSTAND. "Get out of there this instant. I'll wire money anywhere you say. You can't stay there, Em. Are you insane?"

Emma did not have the answer to that question. "At first I was going to leave, but now I can't. Mackie has an ear infection and Ruth's arthritis is acting up. They need me."

"You need a qualified psychiatric examination."

"I need to earn money," she returned, stretching the phone cord across the kitchen so Ruth and the girls couldn't overhear. "You know, the way people who don't have rich husbands or wealthy fathers need to earn money?"

"You never told me you had become a house-keeper."

"I knew you'd laugh."

"Sweetie, you've never had to do more than lift a menu," Paula drawled, now sounding more amused than upset. "How on earth are you going to manage?"

"I've done fine so far. And I have enjoyed it." Which was true. "It's better than being home with my father."

"Yes," Paula admitted, "I guess you have a point. He has told the press that you have been ill and the wedding is indefinitely postponed until you are feeling better. There've been some shots in the news of Ken standing on the steps of Mercy Hospital, looking very concerned and tired."

"He's pretending to visit me in the hospital?"

"I would imagine that was your father's idea, don't you? George Grayson would be looking for the sympathy vote." Paula's voice sharpened. "Be careful, though. The tabloids are still sniffing around. The minute you surface the press will go wild. You'd be wise to call your father and have him arrange your homecoming."

"There's not going to be a homecoming and my father disowned me, remember?"

"He'll forgive and forget. Men do. Just put your little tush on an airplane and don't forget to wear sunglasses and a hat so no one knows who you are."

"Paula, I told you I'm not coming home right now. I was going to, but I can't. Matt...needs me."

"Matt."

"The children's father. The rancher."

"I see. You've gone maternal. Are you sleeping with him?"

She crunched the cord between her fingers. "Paula, of course not!"

"He's a creep?"

"No, not at all. He's quite...wonderful." Melissa

entered the room and wrapped her arms around Emma's knees.

"I'm hungry," the child said. "What's for supper?"

"Just a second, honey," she whispered.

Paula's voice rose. "Well, why don't you sleep with him, then? You might as well enjoy your little vacation to the max."

"I'm hanging up now," she warned, stroking Melissa's soft hair. "I can't talk any longer. The kids are hungry."

Paula chuckled. "The kids are hungry. That's priceless!"

"I'll call you next week. And I'll pay you back for these collect calls." Suddenly she didn't feel like talking to her friend any longer. She didn't want to listen to jokes about Matt or her life here on the ranch.

"Em, I'm sorry, I shouldn't have teased," Paula replied. "Just keep in touch."

She unwound the child from her legs so she could walk over to the wall to hang up the telephone. Why don't you sleep with him? As if sex were that casual, that unimportant. She had waited to be in love before she slept with anyone. She'd thought she'd been in love with Ken, but he had postponed making love until their wedding night. He'd said it was romantic to wait.

She might have waited one heck of a long time.

She'd loved Ken as a friend, as a man she'd known all her life, the man her father had approved of her dating, the man who was conveniently a member of her world. But had she loved him as a woman loves a man with whom she intends to spend the rest of her life?

"Emma." Melissa tugged on her hand. "We're hungry."

Emma smiled into those dark eyes that were so like her father's. "I'll bet you are, honey. We're going to have a pizza party tonight. Doesn't that sound like fun?"

"And after can we dance?"

"Yes, after we'll dance. We'll put the ballet music on the stereo and you can show Aunt Ruth how much you've learned." Which should entertain even Ruth, Emma decided. She went over to the window and looked toward the barns. Where was Matt?

He had kissed her. *Tell me what you want,* he'd said.

That had been an easy question. She'd wanted to remain in his arms until she figured out the answer. She watched as a familiar form strode toward the house. He was coming home for dinner and she would tell him that she was going to stay for as long as he needed her. And whether he liked it or not, he was going to have pizza for supper.

"I'M NOT STAYING TO EAT." Matt went to the coffeepot and poured himself some old coffee. He could have had fresh coffee in the bunkhouse, but he told himself he needed to come back to the house and check on Mackie. "The weather's changing and we're rounding up steers for the sale barn next week. How's Mackie doing?"

Emma opened a jar of tomato sauce and poured some on pizza crusts. "She's fine. Go see for yourself."

He peered around the corner to see all three of his daughters mesmerized by something on television. Ruth gave him a little wave, but turned her attention back to the program immediately. So much for checking in on the family. None of them could be bothered with saying hello. He turned back to Emma and leaned against the counter. "They haven't had television for months. I guess they missed it."

"I won't let them watch too much of it," she promised, "but it's keeping Mackie and Ruth content."

"No small accomplishment," he said and noticed she smiled a little. Did that mean she wasn't angry about this afternoon? He'd said some pretty rough things. And he'd kissed her again, despite his promise not to. She must think he was a sex-starved maniac. He watched her sprinkle cheese on top of the tomato sauce. "I guess I'm going to miss a pretty good supper tonight."

"I'll save you some."

"Don't bother. I'll fix a sandwich in the bunk-house." It would be better that way, he told himself. "I heard you tell Ruth that you're not leaving tomorrow."

"Yes. I mean, no. I'm not leaving." She looked up at him and stopped decorating the pizza. "If it's all right with you, I've decided I'd like to keep working for a while."

It was more than all right. It meant he had another chance. For what he wasn't sure, but he felt a heck of a lot better now.

TWENTY-FOUR HOURS LATER, Emma wasn't so sure she'd made the right decision. Ruth was still in a prone position on the couch, the girls had danced in their ballet shoes until Emma had grown dizzy watching them, and Matt hadn't spent more than five minutes inside the house. Sunday was almost over; she wanted a hot bath, a good book and a quiet evening without the conversation and antics of three little girls and one seventy-something-year-old crochet addict.

Mackie eyed the spoon filled with medicine and shook her head.

"Chocolate shakes, remember?" Emma prompted, one step closer to a hot bath. The little girl opened her mouth and another crisis was averted.

"Good girl," Ruth agreed, who had the amazing abilities to crochet while she was lying flat on her back, carry on a conversation with anyone who would listen and solve the "Wheel of Fortune" puzzle before a contestant bought a vowel. "Martha, hand me some of that blue yarn. I think it's time to change colors."

"Then you and Melissa go upstairs and start getting ready for bed," Emma told them. She'd seen Mel yawn three times and it wasn't even seven o'clock.

"I love this color," Melissa said, touching the rectangle that would soon grow to afghan size. "Yellow like eggs, right, Emma?"

"Yes." The inch-wide strip was the pale yellow color of scrambled eggs. The two oldest girls kissed their aunt good-night and ran upstairs while Emma sat down in the overstuffed chair and pulled Mackie onto her lap. The child's skin was cool and she snuggled against Emma's chest.

Ruth Tuttle shook her head. "I don't know where she gets these ideas," she said.

"Maybe she'll be an artist some day."

"Hard to say, I guess," the woman muttered. "We've never had an artist in the family, but I suppose there's a first time for everything. Those runzas of yours were pretty good, Emma. They really hit the spot."

Emma couldn't hide her surprise. "You liked them?"

"Well, why wouldn't I? Where'd you get the recipe?"

"From the church cookbook." Although the lady who'd contributed the recipe hadn't said it would take hours to make them and there would be enough to feed a football team. "I had no idea it would make that many."

"Better wrap up some for Matt. I'll bet the boy hasn't eaten all day."

"I think he's very busy. He said something last night about selling cattle and how the weather's changing."

"Ranching's always busy work. And lonely, too."

"Matt doesn't seem to mind." He certainly acted as if he couldn't wait to leave the house every morning. And he took his time about coming back inside at night. If it weren't for his daughters, Emma figured the man would sleep in the barn. Mackie tucked her head underneath Emma's chin and closed her eyes.

"Matt minds being alone more than anybody," Ruth declared, lifting her crocheting and holding it toward the light as if she couldn't figure out what color she was using. "Haven't you noticed that yet?"

"Why are you being nice to me, Ruth?"

The old woman shrugged. "Guess I appreciate

your taking care of me like you are. Not many women would put up with an old lady with poor legs."

"You're not that bad."

"I'm not that good, either. I'm a cranky old woman who should mind her own business, but I can't keep my mouth shut and it's too late to start learning how to now. I worry about Matt and I worry about these little girls."

"I would, too," she agreed, "if they were mine."

"It's not easy, raising kids and working on a ranch," Ruth cautioned. "But it's a darn fine life just the same."

"Yes," she said, enjoying the weight of the sleeping child against her arms. "I would imagine it is."

SHE BROUGHT HIM dinner and a thermos of fresh coffee. Wrapped in one of his old jackets, wearing a faded cap with Sowder's General Store written above the brim, Emma had raindrops on her cheeks and mud stuck to whoever's boots she'd borrowed from the mudroom.

"Thanks," was all he could manage to say when she handed him the foil-wrapped package. He hadn't expected she'd find him in the barn tonight. He'd watched the lights go on in the house and he'd wanted to call it a day and head for home, but he hadn't left the building. He could smell the scent of fresh-baked bread. "You didn't have to do this."

"Oh. I guess you already ate in the bunkhouse."

"No. I just meant you didn't have to come out here and deliver my dinner. I don't expect you to worry about things like that, especially right now. And it was supposed to be your day off, too."

She shivered a little. "You haven't been inside very long today."

"I checked on Mackie twice," he said, wondering if she was criticizing what kind of a father he was. "She was doing just fine."

"I meant I know you're busy with the cattle or the weather or something. And Ruth thought you might be hungry, so I thought— Well, anyway, the men said you were in here somewhere, and you'd better eat before those runzas get cold."

"Come sit down where it's warmer," he said, waving her toward the tack room. There were seats in there and the space was fairly clean most of the time. "I guess the girls are in bed?"

"Yes. And Ruth is watching a movie. She's a little better today, but she can't get up and down without help. Have you thought about getting her a walker?"

"Yes. And she scolded until my ears rang." He closed the door behind them to keep the heat in. "Threatened to beat me with her cane, too, so I backed off. I have a strong sense of self-preservation."

"It smells good in here."

"Saddle soap and liniment," he explained. "Have a seat."

She sat down on an old bentwood chair and Matt took the one across from her. "You'd better eat those before they get cold," she said again, looking more like a model than a sand-hills housekeeper. Despite her odd outfit, she was still beautiful. Looks like that couldn't be hidden, even underneath old caps and ancient jackets.

"All right." He peeled back the foil wrapping and picked up a square of dough.

"Even Ruth liked them. She actually said something nice to me tonight."

"Really? Guess she's coming around. No reason why she shouldn't, not with her depending on you for everything."

"I don't mind. I'm getting used to her."

"She's a good-hearted woman, but she can be real outspoken sometimes." He bit into his supper. Not at all bad, considering the woman didn't know how to cook two weeks ago. "This is real good," he said, after he'd swallowed.

"Here." She poured coffee into the lid of the thermos and handed it to him.

"Thanks. You're not having any?"

"No. It would keep me awake. I don't know how you drink as much of that as you do and actually fall asleep at night."

Because he drove himself to work hard eighteen hours a day. When he was working he wasn't thinking about anything but making the ranch work, making the business earn a profit, putting money aside for the girls' educations and paying off loans. He wasn't thinking about Emma and the scent of roses that clung to her skin. Not all of the time.

"Thank you for staying," he said, for lack of anything else to say to her. She sat on the old chair like a princess would, all straight spine and glowing skin. She took off the cap and her hair fell in a sleek motion to her chin. She unbuttoned the jacket to reveal a white T-shirt and slim jeans. There was a spot of mustard on her shirt beneath the collarbone which Matt longed to touch.

He should know better.

"This is a really good runza."

"Yes, you said that." She looked around the room, at the rough wood walls covered with bridles, halters and various leather paraphernalia. She didn't know what half of it was used for. "You must have a lot of horses here."

"We used to have more. My father used horses much more than I do. This isn't the tack we use every day. Do you ride?"

"Not very well. And not since I was twelve."

"I guess I should have asked you that when you first came. You might have wanted to ride once in a while."

She shook her head. "I've always been a little afraid of horses. My riding is even worse than my cooking."

"And your cooking is improving." He finished the rest of the runza in two bites, folded the foil over the others and left the package on the makeshift bench. "Come on. There's someone you should meet."

He led her out of the tack room and through a long corridor down one side of the barn. The rain pounded on the metal roof, so he had to speak above the noise when he reached Cody.

"Here he is," Matt announced, stopping in front of the stall. "Bill Cody, oldest horse on the place. We keep him in the barn at night to keep those old bones of his warm." The palomino hung his head over the top bar to have his nose rubbed. "Hey, boy, how ya doin'?" Matt turned to Emma, who looked intrigued but uncertain. "Go ahead. He won't bite."

"Are you sure?"

"Yeah." He watched her tentatively stroke old Cody's nose. "See? He likes the attention. The girls bring him apples and carrots in the winter, but he spends his summer in a nearby pasture. I just brought him inside yesterday."

"So he's safe and warm for the winter?"

"Yes. My father would have wanted Cody to be well taken care of."

Emma's expression changed and she withdrew her hand. "I should get back to the house."

"You'll be soaked." The rain pounded so loud that he had to raise his voice. "Wait till it lets up. If Ruth needs anything she'll call the bunkhouse. She'll tell Jasper where you are. Can she reach the phone?"

"I put the extension on the floor next to her."

Matt nodded, pleased that she was his for a while longer. "Then let me give you a tour."

"You have the time?"

"Lady, I have all the time in the world." He winked, hoping to make her smile again, but her lips turned up only a little bit. "Is something wrong?"

"Your father," she began. "Were you very close?"

"Yeah. I worked beside him from the time I could walk. So did my sister Stephanie, but she wanted to leave the ranch and all I wanted to do was stay here for the rest of my life." She still looked sad, so Matt pointed to a crude ladder nailed to the wall. "You ever been up in a haymow, city lady?"

She brightened. "Oh, so you're calling me names now that you've had your supper."

"Come on." He put one booted foot on the ladder. "I'll go first so I can help you up. The top step's a little tricky."

"Okay. I guess there's a first time for everything."

He climbed the ladder with ease, then knelt over the opening to take her hand if she needed help. He ended up with his hands under her arms, half lifting her into the loft, but he released her the second she caught her balance and stood on a small section of space that wasn't covered with hay. "I saw rolls of hay in fields on my way to town," Emma said. "I didn't know you kept it in barns, too."

"We bale enough for the horses and some of the calves that we keep close to home," he explained. He looked up at the roof. "The rain's really coming down hard now."

"It smells good up here. The way a barn should smell." She sat down on a hay bale and surveyed the enormous space. A half-grown yellow cat appeared and rubbed himself against Emma's legs. "Hi, kitty." She stroked the animal's back and looked at Matt. "How did he get up here?"

Matt smiled. "There's a set of stairs in the back of the barn."

"And you made me climb a ladder."

"I thought you should have the experience," he said, defending himself. "Climbing a hayloft is better than walking up into one."

She laughed. The sound startled the cat and sent it scampering up a mountain of bales. "I'm glad I don't have to climb down. I'm better at going up than going down."

"You don't have to go anywhere." The words took on more meaning than he intended, but he found he couldn't look away.

"I couldn't leave you, not with a sick child and Ruth not feeling well. It wouldn't have been fair."

"People do a lot of things that aren't fair."

"Not me," she said, raising her chin in a way he'd begun to recognize.

"No," he said, "Not you." He motioned toward the back of the barn. "We'd better get going. We shouldn't be out here alone anyway."

"Shouldn't?" She smiled at him, echoing his words from yesterday.

"This is a mistake," he said, stepping close enough to see those green eyes of hers widen. He took her hand and tugged her toward the stairs.

"Yes," she agreed. "A very big mistake."

"Mistakes happen," he whispered, drawing her to him. And somehow his arms were around Emma, his mouth tasted the sweet warmth of hers and together the two of them tumbled down into the fragrant hay. He could no more stop himself than he could stop the rain pounding on the roof above them, especially when her fingers caressed his face and tangled in his hair, holding his mouth to hers in a kiss that could wait no longer.

He kissed the warm skin above her collarbone, slid his hand along the soft cotton shirt until he cupped her breast.

"Matt," she said, gasping a little as his thumb caressed the bud of her nipple. "There's something—"

He touched his mouth to the edge of her bottom lip. "Anyone ever tell you how soft your mouth is?"

"No. Which is what—"

After another long kiss, he lifted his mouth from hers. "Emma?"

She opened her eyes. "What?"

"Tell me this isn't a mistake."

Emma ran one finger down the length of his cheek and brushed it across his lips. "I don't think it feels like one, but I've made a lot of them lately so I can't really be sure."

"Me, too," Matt murmured, tucking her warm body beneath his. "I guess we'll just have to take our chances."

"Okay." She smiled at him and Matt felt the tightness around his heart ease. She wanted him, too—a miracle here on this rainy Sunday night. "Kiss me again," Emma said. "So far that's my favorite part."

He couldn't help smiling. "Lady, you might be in for a few surprises. Kissing is just the beginning."

"I've heard that." Her gaze didn't waver as she looked into his eyes. "You'll have to teach me the rest."

It took a second to sink in, but Emma's uncertain expression finally penetrated his skull. "You mean you've never—"

"No. Never."

"Your fiancé—"

"Wanted to wait."

The man must have been as cold as ice, Matt figured, but he didn't want to think about the other man that Emma had loved. For all he knew she still did. Women were strange creatures and sometimes had odd notions. "Good" was all Matt could say. "I haven't made love with anyone in a long, long time," he admitted, brushing her lips with his. "We'll just have to practice together until we get it right."

10

SOMEHOW THEY MANAGED to remove their clothes, though Emma wasn't quite sure how their jackets became a bed in the hay. The sensation of Matt's bare chest against her breasts drove all thought from her mind. She turned into a happy, trembling mass of heated skin and melting bones. Matt caressed her with his fingertips, sending shivers of anticipation through her, and she reached for him with a matching, insistent touch.

He didn't ask her again if she was sure she wanted to make love. Emma didn't think he had to, not when her body was as eager as his, not when he tilted her on her side facing him and she ended up sprawled on top of him. She looked down into his dark eyes and saw someone whom she could trust. "It gets better than this?" she teased.

Matt tucked a strand of her hair behind her ear. "Yeah. We haven't gotten to the best part yet."

"Really." She leaned down and kissed his chin. "So, when do we do that?"

"I thought you'd never ask." He eased her onto her back.

Emma couldn't help smiling. "I didn't know I was supposed to."

"It helps," he said, caressing her with a slow motion. His hand palmed her abdomen, then lower, until she couldn't bear the pleasure his fingers were giving her any longer.

"Now," she said, reaching to hold him as he settled himself above her.

His words were soft against her ear. "I'm going to try not to hurt you."

"You won't."

And he didn't, at least, not for more than an instant. There was the briefest pain, followed by the sense of being opened. Being filled. Being completed. And when he moved gently within her, she held on to Matt's broad shoulders and wondered that anything could feel so right.

Matt stayed deep within her as he looked into her face. "Are you okay?"

"Yes. You feel good inside me." She moved her hips to bring him deeper, and Matt winced.

"Don't get fancy, sweetheart," he groaned. "It's been a long time since anything felt this good and I'd like it to last more than sixty seconds."

"Show me more," she whispered, taking him deeper inside her. He moved within her with deep strokes, over and over until the pleasure built to the point of pain. She climaxed suddenly, a fragile internal explosion that was answered by Matt's faster strokes and deep shuddering thrusts. He moved within her until he was empty, until his breathing grew slower and he lowered himself onto her body. He moved to his side, taking her with him, and stroked her back with lazy fingers.

"We're crazy," he said after a long moment.

"Why do you say that?" His touch was heaven against her shoulder blades. She closed her eyes.

"We didn't use anything. And I'm old enough to know better than to take risks like that."

"I'm on the pill," she murmured, trying not to feel hurt by the phrase *old enough to know better*. "I was supposed to get married, remember? And he didn't want children right away." She hoped he wouldn't ask how long ago she'd broken her engagement.

Matt sighed and kissed her shoulder. "There are other reasons to use protection, Emma."

"Yes, but I'm—was—a virgin and you said you've been celibate." She opened her eyes and looked at him. He frowned. "You didn't lie about that, did you?"

"No, of course not, but you can't go around having sex without using a condom, Emma. Some men do lie. And will. From now on, you—"

"From now on? You think I'm going to start making love—excuse me, you said 'having sex,' didn't you—with anyone?" She scooted back, briefly regretting the sudden loss of his body from inside hers, and reached for her clothes. "This was supposed to be special."

"It was," he said, frowning again as he sat up and brushed bits of hay from his hair. "Very special, especially for someone who hasn't—"

"I didn't make love with you out of curiosity, because I hadn't done it before." She found her T-shirt and, not bothering to put on her bra, pulled it over her head.

"I was talking about myself," he admitted, sliding his arms into the sleeves of his plaid shirt. "I haven't been with a woman since Patty died. That's all I was going to say. That it was special for me, too."

She didn't know why her eyes filled with tears, but she didn't want Matt to see her cry. She didn't want him to know how much the experience meant to her. For him it was a release. For her it was...love.

"I'd better go," she said, grabbing her jeans and tugging them on. Matt picked up her underwear and bra and handed them to her. She didn't look at him, but shoved the clothing into the jacket pocket, then found her socks and boots and struggled to tug them on.

"It's still raining real hard," he said, as if she couldn't hear the rain pounding the roof like pellets.

"A little water won't hurt me."

"Be careful, Emma," he said, sounding worried.

"That's one heck of a storm we've got going. I'd better walk you back to the house."

"No," she said, finally dressed. "Don't bother. I'm tougher than I look."

"At least let me take you to the stairs," he said, carefully stepping away from her. He led her down the back stairs and through the barn to the front door. He put his hand on her arm and stopped her from leaving. "Emma," he said, forcing her to look at him. "I'm sorry."

"Me, too." She headed out into the rain toward the house. The spotlight in front of the barn lit most of the yard, until she was on the other side of the rise and the lights in the kitchen showed her the rest of the way. The tears she'd managed to suppress spilled over onto her cheeks and mingled with the September rain. She was in love with him. She had made love with him. And that wonderful, passionate experience had been a mistake after all.

She should have left when she had the chance.

"'ACHY BREAKY HEART,'" Aunt Ruth announced, shaking her head at the television. "I wish they'd make them puzzles harder. That was an easy one, I declare." She picked up her crocheting and started working the hook back and forth. "Buy an *a*, you fools."

Martha sat on the floor and leaned against the

back of the couch. "I don't think they're kissing any more."

"Who?"

"Daddy and Emma."

"Oh. Well, honey, folks don't always spend their time kissing, you know."

She turned and rested her chin on the couch cushion. She sure hoped Aunt Ruth would know what to do. "Daddy's not smiling anymore. And Emma looks out the window a lot."

"My goodness, Martha, you're sure keeping an eye on things around here, aren't you?"

"Don't you see? Emma's gonna leave if we don't do something."

"Emma's not leaving. She's making ballerina costumes for you for Halloween. The poor gal can't sew for beans, but she's figuring it out. I guess you're gonna wear those fancy shoes, too."

Martha didn't want to talk about her ballet slippers. She wanted help. "The party's a long way away. Maybe she's making them now 'cuz she's not gonna be here."

Aunt Ruth set her afghan in her lap and sighed one of her big, heavy sighs. "Martha, you have old eyes."

"What does that mean?"

"Means those eyes of yours see too much. If Emma wants to leave, there ain't nothing we can do about it. And if your daddy wanted to spend more time kissing and less time working outside, well, that's what he would do."

"They'd kiss if they were alone. Just like they did before."

"They're not gonna be alone with three kids and an old woman underfoot." Martha frowned and glanced toward "Wheel of Fortune." "Oh, drat. It's one of those new Before-and-After puzzles."

"My teacher says that if you walk the riverbeds now you can find stuff."

"What's that got to do with kissing?"

Martha shrugged. "We could all go for a walk. I'll bet Emma's never found any arrowheads or dinosaur bones before."

"And?"

"Daddy could come, too." And she would figure out a way to keep Mel and Mackie from bothering them. They would be alone. They would kiss. And Daddy would smile again and Emma's eyes wouldn't be all puffy and red.

"Well," Aunt Ruth declared, poking through her yarn bag. "I guess you've got yourself a plan. If you don't mind, I'll stay here on the couch and work on this afghan."

"Good idea," Martha agreed. "I'll go tell Emma we're going on a picnic tomorrow."

"Where'd she go?"

"She's giving Mel a bath, I think."

"I hope she doesn't miss 'Jeopardy,'" Aunt Ruth said. "We always have our tea and see who gets the most answers right."

Martha scooted away from the couch and hurried upstairs. Emma would love a treasure hunt.

"HOLD MACKIE'S HAND," Emma cautioned the older girls. "And don't get too close to the mud."

They ran off ahead, their giggles floating through the cool afternoon air. Matt didn't know how he'd gotten talked into this, but he didn't really mind spending the last Saturday walking along the dried-up riverbeds. Especially when he was walking beside Emma, who might even have to talk to him. If she fell into a hole she would have to yell for help. Not that he wanted her to hurt herself, but she'd have to talk to him then, damn it. She hadn't said a thing to him for almost two weeks except to ask, "Do you want any more of this coffee or should I throw it out?" or "Please pass the potatoes."

He'd been trying to talk to her and she'd been trying to pretend he didn't exist. Lately he'd wondered what he'd have to do to get her alone.

"My father used to stop and look for arrowheads along this river," Matt said, hoping that Emma would say something. Anything.

"Did he find any?"

That was a start. Matt took a deep breath and tried not to jinx himself. "Yeah. A few. There were Pawnee settlements in this area for a few hundred years. And every so often some archaeology professor from Doane College will come out and ask permission to look for dinosaur bones."

"That's what Martha told me," Emma said, "but I really didn't know whether or not to believe her."

"She's been to Morrill Hall and seen the dinosaurs there at the university. Fossil hunting is better in early November, though, before the ground is frozen hard." Matt tossed a stick for Sorrow, whom the kids had insisted on taking with them. Matt hadn't protested; the old dog could use the exercise, especially after Emma had attempted to make beef stroganoff on Thursday.

"What do you think we'll find?"

"Maybe some crockery from pioneers, maybe some old bones." The dog ran back panting and dropped the stick of driftwood at Matt's feet. "Maybe nothing."

"Oh, they'll discover something," Emma said. "Pretty rocks or bright leaves. Girls are good at that."

"You're finally talking to me," he said, tossing the stick again. It made a wide arc in the cloudless sky and the dog barked with excitement. "I appreciate it. Does this mean you're going to let me apologize?"

"I really don't want—"

"To talk about it," he finished for her. Matt stopped and turned toward her. "Well, we're talking about it. Now. We made love two weeks ago, Emma."

"Is that what it was? I thought it was 'having sex.'"

He took her arm as she started to walk away. "It was making love, Emma. And it was very special. I never meant to hurt you." He bent over and brushed her lips with his.

"You shouldn't do that," she said, but she didn't look too upset. "The girls could see."

"They're too busy looking at rocks to notice." He smiled. "Am I forgiven?"

Emma didn't return the smile. "This is very awkward."

"It doesn't have to be." Though for the past thirteen days, whenever he looked at her, he'd remembered being inside her. He'd remembered the taste of her skin and how tight she'd been around him. Every time he walked into the barn he got hard. And every time he reminded himself that he had no business mooning around after Emma, he didn't listen. She was a city woman, she was here only temporarily, she was not his type. And yet, he was standing here looking at her and wanting to kiss her again, only he didn't want to be standing up the next time it happened.

"I think we should just stay away from each other." But she let him take her hand and lead her along the riverbank. "I think that's been working very well so far."

"I think we should go out to dinner," he countered. "Just the two of us. You must be tired of cooking."

She almost smiled. "You must be tired of eating my cooking."

"Sweetheart, that dog and I have eaten everything you've come up with." Sorrow bounded back and ran circles around them.

"Are you asking me out on a date?"

He swallowed and hoped he would answer the right way. "Yeah, I think it's about time. Don't you?"

"Daddy!" Melissa came running toward them with something in her hand. "Look what I found!" Emma tugged her hand from his as his daughter approached. "But I don't know what it is." She dropped it into his hand. "What do you think it could be?"

It was a piece of bone that was preventing him from hearing Emma's reply to his dinner invitation, that's what it was. Matt turned it over in his hand. "I'd say it was a Pawnee tool of some kind, maybe a hoe."

Melissa began jumping up and down, while her sisters called to her. "Really? Can I take it to school?"

"I don't know why not. I think it's probably made out of a buffalo bone, but next time we're in Lincoln we can stop at Morrill Hall and ask."

"Cool!"

He handed it to Emma. "Have you ever seen anything like it?"

"No, I never have." She returned the bone to his daughter. "It's white like bones, isn't it?"

Melissa shook her head. "White like a puzzle. White like the water."

"That little stream is brown. Like mud," Matt said. "How do you figure it's white?"

His daughter sighed. "Sometimes it's white when the sun is on it."

"Oh." She was going to be an artist, Emma said. Matt guessed they saw things differently, because that stream bed was nothing but brown.

"That's incredible that you found something," Emma told her. "Show me where."

"Okay." This time it was his daughter who took Emma's hand. Matt stood by the riverbank and watched them run back to where the others were hunched over a mound of dirt beneath a clump of cottonwood trees.

He'd worried that Emma would leave once Mackie's earache ended, but instead she'd stayed. It wasn't because of him—he didn't fool himself into thinking it was—but Emma knew that Ruth couldn't manage the girls by herself. His aunt remained on the couch and hobbled back and forth to the kitchen to eat, but he knew she was in pain. He figured Emma knew it, too. But what would happen when Ruth moved back to her house and Emma was free to go?

Matt hurried to join his family. He would eventually find someone to take care of the girls, he knew. But replacing Emma wouldn't be easy.

Even thinking about it made him break into a sweat.

EMMA WAITED ALL WEEK to decide for sure, though on Sunday she'd taken some of the money she'd saved and driven to North Platte to buy a dress. She couldn't go out to dinner—if that's what she decided to do—wearing her jeans and a T-shirt. She bought a pale green cardigan sweater to match the ankle-length knit, too. And still had plenty left over to buy a plane ticket to Chicago, which she would have to do eventually.

She'd asked for information at the small airport in North Platte, just to make sure.

The rest of the week was the same as always. Emma shuttled the girls back and forth to school, bought groceries, cooked meals and even—when given no choice—grabbed the vacuum cleaner and went over the rugs. Mackie talked incessantly about her upcoming birthday, Martha's friend came over one afternoon to practice ballet, and she'd joined two mothers for coffee at Stu's one morning while pre-school was in session. She still fell exhausted into bed by nine-thirty, but she no longer wept when a meal didn't turn out right.

The Thomsons ate it anyway.

"You're gonna miss the show!"

"Coming!" Emma hurried downstairs after putting Mackie and Melissa in bed for their afternoon quiet time. She rounded the corner of the living room and took her place in the chair facing the television. Ruth had explained "Days of Our Lives" to her and now she was as hooked as Ruth.

"Here," Ruth said, handing her a rectangle of what might end up as an afghan sometime in the next millennium. "I went back and fixed that hole, and I untangled the green yarn so when you feel like changing colors, you can tie on the green."

"Thank you." She'd never made anything before, unless she counted the embroidered napkins in Miss Finch's home skills class. Miss Finch wouldn't have survived three hours in Nebraska. "I really appreciate your teaching me how to crochet."

"Can't believe you never tried before. You'll get

the hang of it, when you start getting your pointer finger going right."

Emma arranged the yarn in her lap, then picked up the crochet hook. "Did you take your medicine?"

"I forgot." Ruth winced and reached for her pills. "I thought I'd be better by now, Emma. I hate to be any trouble."

"You're not," she assured Ruth. "Besides, you have to stay until I get the hang of crocheting."

Ruth sighed. "Well, I guess that means I'm gonna be here one heck of a long time then. Are you?"

Emma's smile faded when she met the woman's gaze. "I don't think so."

"Got a reason?"

"Yes. A few." An angry father. A life in Chicago. A deceitful ex-fiancé. And a rancher who would never love her, who thought that she would make love to other men someday. Well, maybe he was right, but she couldn't imagine touching another man when she'd fallen in love with Matt Thomson.

"Hope they're good ones," Ruth said, staring at the television screen. "What do you think of Marlena's daughter canceling her wedding like that?"

"I think she did the right thing." Emma looped a strand of yellow yarn around her finger and stuck the crochet hook into what she hoped was the right place.

"Yeah, well, a woman ought to be sure of her man before she walks down the aisle, that's what I say."

"You're a wise woman," Emma agreed.

"Honey, when you've been married three times like I have, you'd better be smart. And you'd better know men."

Emma thought of Matt and how he'd asked her out to dinner. "How can you ever understand men?"

"Sex and food, for starters." Ruth cackled. "That's what makes 'em tick. That and protecting their womenfolk. You've got to make a man feel like he's the king of the mountain, like he's special."

"How do you do that?" The ball of green yarn tumbled off her lap and dropped onto the floor.

"If he's a good man, you feed him, you love him, and you treat him kindly. Some of them aren't too smart, but they all have feelings." Ruth shifted position and winced. "Hand me that scissors, will you? I'm getting tired of purple."

She'd tell him yes, Emma decided. Besides, it had been weeks since she'd had the pleasure of ordering from a menu.

MATT WAITED for her in the living room. When Emma entered the room, he stood and smiled at her.

"I'm ready," she announced, wondering why everyone was staring at her. "What's the matter?"

"You—you look beautiful," he stammered.

Melissa scurried over and touched the flaring skirt. "It's green like apples."

"That's what the lady in the store called it. Apple green."

"Where's the princess dress?" Martha looked disappointed. "I thought you were going to wear it tonight."

"I like this dress much better," Emma assured her. "And white isn't appropriate for this time of year."

"I like your boots, though," Martha said. "My teacher has some like that."

Emma looked down at the rounded toes of her cream-colored Western boots. "I couldn't resist. They were on sale."

"Very nice," Matt said. "We'll make a Western woman out of you yet."

She wiggled her toes against the leather. "They're more comfortable than I thought they'd be."

"Come on, then. We're going to town." He took her hand and she couldn't resist curling her fingers around his. He gave her fingers a gentle squeeze and tugged her toward the door while she gave instructions for bedtimes and snacks and television shows.

"Nothing scary," she insisted. "And bedtime at nine o'clock."

"No problem," Martha said, beaming at them. "Have a good time."

Emma had a wonderful time. She told herself it

was because she didn't have to cook dinner. Because she had a waiter and a menu and a candle-lit table.

Not because she was in love and the man she loved was seated across from her. Oh, no. And being in love with him didn't mean that he needed to know. In fact, it was a lot better for her that he didn't know. Her pride had taken a beating lately. She didn't need a cowboy to stomp all over it now.

THEIR BOOTS HIT the floor at the same time.

"Oh, that feels good," Emma moaned, reaching for her battered toes. "I'll never get used to them."

"Lie down," Matt said, and Emma leaned back on his wide bed while Matt rubbed her feet. "Better?"

"Much better. I never had this much trouble wearing high heels. I thought boots were supposed to be comfortable."

"You have to break them in," he murmured, stroking her leg. He lifted the hem of her dress and planted a kiss on the inside of her knee. "You have to go slow, take it a little at a time."

Emma felt the warmth spread from her knees upward, as Matt's hands stroked higher and higher. "Are you talking about wearing boots or doing something else?"

"You can't do too much at once," he said, ignoring her question. "Not if you expect to be able to walk the next day."

She looked up at the ceiling. "What am I doing in here?"

His lips traced a trail up her thigh. "I think that's pretty obvious, sweetheart."

"When you call me 'sweetheart' I know I'm in trouble." She felt his fingers skim over her panties.

"We're both in trouble," he said. "Have been since you looked at me in The Golden Corral."

"True." There had been something about being alone together that made them both think of sex. They'd skipped dessert. He'd driven the truck eighty miles an hour all the way home. She gasped as he slid his hand along her abdomen and tugged the underwear down her legs. "Do all the restaurants in Nebraska have such original names?"

Her dress was around her waist, her panties had joined her boots and socks on the floor, and Matt's lips were teasing the inside of her thigh. She wondered if anyone ever fainted from sheer pleasure. Matt eased her thighs apart and touched his lips to a place made so sensitive by his touch that she bit her lips to keep from making a sound.

"Let me love you like this," he said, before his mouth was against her, taking her to a place where all feeling centered on what Matt was doing to her with his lips and his tongue. His hands held her thighs apart, his mouth drove her to peak after peak of pleasure until she could hold back no longer. Sensation, hot and surprising, burst inside her. Matt continued to kiss her, moving slower until every last bit of energy had drained from her body. He left her then; she heard him remove his clothes, felt the bed dip as he got in on the other side.

"Come on, sweetheart, I'll help you take off your dress."

"You've done enough," she managed to whisper, but she struggled to sit up and pull the dress over her head.

"We've only begun," he said, touching his finger to her lace-covered breast. Emma removed her bra and tossed that over the edge of the bed, too. She scooted under the covers to face him and smoothed her hand along his side and lower, to touch the hard, hot length of him.

She smiled at Matt's groan of pleasure. "What happens next?"

He kissed her and then smiled. "Sweetheart, as long as you don't get out of this bed, you'll find out."

11

"I DO BELIEVE I'm feeling better," Ruth declared, lifting herself off the couch. "That was a nasty spell. Do you want help frosting that cake?"

"I'm all set," Emma assured her. "I bought a couple of cans of chocolate frosting."

Ruth blanched. "Cans?"

Emma tucked her future afghan—all seven inches of it—into the plastic bag that held her yarn. "Days of Our Lives" was over and Mackie would soon wake from her nap. "Where'd Melissa go? She said she wanted to help decorate the cake."

"You're a brave one," Ruth muttered. "She'll have you both covered in chocolate by the time you're done."

Emma looked down at her spotted jeans. "That's okay. I already made a mess baking the darn thing."

Ruth shook her head. "You've never made a cake before, have you?"

"No, but the cookbook—"

"You've got grit, girl. I'll say that for you." She grabbed her cane and hobbled stiffly across the room to the front porch. "Never thought you'd last a week."

Neither did I. Emma retrieved the birthday girl from her bed, gave her a quick bath and dressed her in her prettiest dress.

"I'm four," Mackie said, holding up four fingers.

"I know." She knelt down and brushed the girl's hair with gentle strokes until it was smooth enough to pull into a ponytail, which was Mackie's favorite hairstyle.

"I get a party at school."

"Yes. Tomorrow. I made cupcakes." So far she'd baked a chocolate layer cake and twenty-three cupcakes. The presents were wrapped, the meat baking in a special casserole and the Jell-O—cherry this time—mixed and refrigerated right after breakfast. She was taking no chances tonight. Nothing would go wrong to spoil the evening.

"You have my present?"

"I do. Turn around and let me see how pretty you look." The child smiled. "I do believe, Miss Mackenzie, that you look like you're four years old."

Mackie threw her arms around Emma's neck. "I love you, Emma."

"I love you, too, honey." Oh, yes, she certainly loved all of them, though this was the first time she'd said the words aloud. Matt was loving and generous in many ways, but he didn't talk about the future. He worked hard all day, but sometimes he asked her to ride with him in the truck when he wanted company. She drove the girls to town, made some friends, bought the groceries. Her afghan grew and so did the love she felt for her new family. He never mentioned love and neither did she. They held each other in the darkness, which was enough. For now.

Maybe, since Matt was stopping work early tonight, he would come to her bed. They'd slept together often these past weeks, either in his room or hers. She smiled to herself. There were advantages to being the last ones to go to bed at night and the first ones awake in the morning.

"Come on," she told the little girl. "Let's go get ready for your party. You can't peek in the kitchen, though."

"Is my cake pretty?"

"It will be, as soon as Melissa and I get done with it," she promised. "Aunt Ruth is out on the porch. You can play there and watch for Martha to come home."

It should have been simple, Emma thought later, except the frosting stuck and lifted off chunks of cake if she didn't hold the butter knife at the perfect angle. There was a lot of trial and error before the perfect angle was discovered. Melissa preferred to dip her fingers in the frosting, which occupied her quite well until Emma saw the child's face and clothes. One of the cats mysteriously got into the house and had to be chased outside. Ruth forgot where she'd hidden Mackie's birthday present, Martha became teary when she remembered she'd left her sister's "special card" in her desk at school, and Matt came in for coffee and tracked heaven-knew-what across the clean kitchen floor.

She handed him a broom. "You brought it in. You take it out."

"Yes, ma'am." He winked at her, made Martha smile and swiped some frosting when he thought Emma wasn't looking. Of course she was looking; she loved looking at him.

"Stop it right now," she ordered, which made the girls giggle.

"You have chocolate right here," he said, touching Emma's cheek. His eyes sparkled with mischief, so Emma automatically lifted her chin so he could kiss her.

"Auntie Steph!" Martha screeched, and Matt turned around as a tall brunette stood in the doorway of the kitchen. The stunned expression on her face showed that she'd seen her brother standing too close to the housekeeper. Emma took a step back and met the woman's gaze. She wore her hair in a carefully rumpled chin-length shag, her tan trousers were expensive linen, and her white blouse was open at the neck to reveal a thick gold necklace. She carried a leather coat over one arm, her purse in her hand, and a chip on her shoulder.

"Hello," Matt's sister said, her glance taking in Emma's rumpled clothes and chocolate-stained fingers. Martha and Melissa hugged their aunt and jumped up and down. Stephanie appeared to take it in stride. She turned back to Emma and gave her a polite smile. "I'm Stephanie Cordell, Matt's sister."

"What are you doing here?" Matt gave Emma the broom and threw his arm around his sister's shoulders. "Steph, meet Emma Gray, the new housekeeper who saved my life."

The new housekeeper? Emma wasn't sure she cared for that phrase, but she supposed Matt couldn't say "Meet my new lover" in front of the children. She plastered a smile on her face and shook the hand that Stephanie so coolly offered. "Hi," she said. "I'm glad to meet you. The girls have talked so much about—"

"I didn't hear a car pull in," Ruth said, her face breaking into a smile as she greeted her niece. "Oh, Lord, I should have known you wouldn't miss Mackie's birthday."

"Auntie Steph?" Mackie ran into her arms.

"Happy birthday, honey." She handed her a big box wrapped in pink teddy bear paper and turned to Ruth to give her a careful hug. "Clay had to be in Denver for a business meeting, so I had him drop me off to surprise you all." Her glance flickered over Emma again.

"Is Clay coming in?" Matt asked.

"I wouldn't let him. I made him drop me off at the end of the drive so you wouldn't see the car."

Matt chuckled. "Some people in this family never grow up."

"And some of us keep secrets," she said, punching him on the arm.

"Hey," he protested. "What was that for?"

Stephanie didn't answer him. She helped Ruth into a kitchen chair. "Matt said you were laid up on the couch. Are you feeling better?"

"Ready to go home tomorrow," Ruth announced, which was news to Emma. Matt looked surprised, too.

"Can I open it?" Mackie asked.

Her aunt smiled. "Sure."

"No," Matt said at the same time.

"Why don't you wait until after you blow out the candles?" Emma asked the child. "It will be so much nicer to open all the presents at once."

"Okay." She struggled past her sisters and put the box on the table. "It looks so pretty. Thank you very, very much."

"You're very, very welcome."

Matt headed toward the hall. "I came in to clean

up for supper, so I'll go do that before I track any more dirt on the floor.

"Good idea," Stephanie said, then turned to Emma and frowned. "Have we met before, Emma?"

"No."

"You look familiar. Have you ever lived in Omaha?"

"No." She leaned the broom against the wall and walked behind the counter. She wished they would leave her alone in the kitchen so she could fix supper without an audience. "Why don't you all go in the living room and let me get dinner on the table. I'll call you when it's ready."

"Come, darlings," their aunt said to the girls. "Let's not get in Emma's way. I'm sure she'd be happier if we left her to her work." Stephanie glanced at the birthday cake, whose top layer listed to one side. "Are you sure you wouldn't like some help?"

"No. Everything's under control," Emma assured her. "We'll eat in about an hour."

"Okay." The girls followed her out of the room, with Ruth hobbling behind as fast as she could go, leaving Emma alone to finish preparing a meal that had to be special. For Mackie's sake.

"INTERESTING FLAVOR, Emma," Matt said, finishing a second helping of the round steak casserole.

"It was very…unusual," his sister agreed. "What's in it?"

"Round steak, green beans, mushroom soup and canned milk." Emma helped Mackie wipe her face with her napkin. So far so good. "The recipe called for evaporated milk, but I couldn't find any so I used sweetened condensed milk instead."

"Really," Stephanie said, exchanging a glance with Ruth. "It was very good."

"Very good," Ruth echoed.

"Can I help you clear?"

"No. Everyone just sit still. We'll have cake and coffee in a few minutes."

"And presents," Mackie declared. "And candles."

"Yes," Emma laughed. "Those, too."

No one seemed to notice that the cake was crooked and had a few bare spots peppering its side. Emma had managed to write Happy Birthday with a tube full of decorative pink frosting, and Mackie blew out four fat pink candles with very little trouble and a great deal of applause. The child opened her presents while Emma tried to cut the cake.

Matt noticed she was having trouble. "What's the matter? Do you want me to sharpen that knife?"

"No." She made a face as she peered at the bottom of the cake. "I used new cake pans, the kind that have the removable sides. I guess I forgot to take the bottom one off."

"It could happen to anyone," Stephanie said. "What did you do before you came to work here?"

She gritted her teeth and managed to slide a piece of cake onto a pink paper plate. "I took care of my father."

"Was he ill?"

"No." He was spoiled and arrogant and accustomed to having his orders obeyed. And she wished they hadn't parted so badly.

"Oh."

A new dress from her aunt, thick jigsaw puzzles from Ruth, a Barbie doll from her sisters, another pink teddy bear from her father and a tiny pink dance leotard and matching tights—ordered from JCPenney—from Emma made Mackie squeal with excitement. The girls hurried off to put on their dance outfits to show Stephanie, and Emma shooed the adults into the living room. She promised them coffee and refused their offers of help. She took a couple of aspirin, wrapped up the last two pieces of cake, gathered the wrapping paper into the garbage, turned on the coffeepot and soaked the dirty dishes. She had survived her first dinner party. She had met Matt's sister.

The world had not come to an end.

"Emma, come see!" Martha ran to the door of the kitchen. "You're on TV!"

She shouldn't have walked into the living room.

She shouldn't have stood beside Matt and watched a video of Emilie Grayson stepping out of a black limousine and onto the sidewalk beside the church.

"The princess dress!" Melissa shouted.

"What on earth—" Stephanie began, but Ruth shushed her.

"Emilie Grayson, the 'Runaway Bride,' is still sequestered in the psychiatric unit of this Chicago hospital," said the announcer. A shot of Ken on the hospital steps replaced the wedding picture. "Her fiancé, Ken Channing, remains a devoted visitor while campaigning for the senate seat vacated by his father. Rumor has it that George Grayson, the bride's father, is a major contributor to Channing's campaign. But where is Emilie Grayson? Last seen on August thirtieth, was she stepping into a taxi? Or admitted to a hospital, rumored to be suffering a breakdown? Or…did the bride just decide she didn't want to be a senator's wife after all? Stay tuned tomorrow for an interview with the woman who designed the bridal gown!"

"I wanted to watch 'Wheel of Fortune,' but the clicker wouldn't work. Darn batteries must have run out," Ruth muttered. She hit the television's control panel with her cane and lowered the volume. "How do you change the channel on this thing?"

"A twin sister," Matt said, turning to Emma. "Tell me she's your twin sister."

"So that's why you look familiar." Stephanie gathered the children to her side as if she needed to protect them from a monster. "You've been on 'Hard Copy' a lot this past month."

Martha looked up at her aunt. "Want to see the princess dress? Emma's got it in her closet."

"Martha, take your sisters upstairs. It's bedtime." Matt didn't take his gaze from Emma's face as the children hurried out of the room. "What the hell is going on here?"

"I couldn't marry him," she whispered. "Remember? I told you I found out my fiancé loved someone else."

"At the wedding?" Stephanie asked, incredulous. "You are Emilie Grayson? No wonder you can't cook. You were on the cover of *Woman's Day* last summer." She turned to Ruth. "They did an entire feature on how to plan a wedding."

Ruth sat down on the couch. "You escaped the nuthouse and came to Nebraska? Whatever for?"

"I was never in a hospital," Emma explained. "That's just a story my father made up. I ran away from the wedding and got on the first plane out of Chicago. It landed in Lincoln."

"You're not Emma Gray," was all Matt could say. "You're some society princess who needed a place to hide for a while. How long were you going to keep this up? Until after the election? Was it that important that your boyfriend get elected?"

"I didn't want to hurt anyone."

His eyebrows rose. "Yeah. I guess people like you are used to getting what you want. Without hurting anyone, of course."

"You don't have to be sarcastic," Stephanie warned. "Maybe Emma was afraid. Why else would she run away and hide?"

"Why else?" Matt echoed. "Who knows why Emma does a lot of things?"

She knew he waited for her to explain, but she didn't know what to say to him in front of the other women. "May I speak with you privately?"

He shook his head. "I don't feel like talking any more." He left the room and minutes later the three women heard the back door slam. Emma gathered up the birthday gifts.

"I guess I'd better take these to Mackie and see that the children get into bed."

"I'll help you," Stephanie offered, lifting the bear from Emma's arms. "I've missed them terribly." She followed Emma up the stairs. "This is for the best, you know. Don't worry. Once you return to your own life, I'll take the children home with me. Matt can't care for them by himself and Ruth can't deal with them, not as active as they are."

"No, of course not." Emma hesitated when she

reached the landing. She turned to Matt's sister. "He didn't want to give you the girls to raise, did he?"

"No." Stephanie's eyes filled up with tears. "My husband and I haven't been able to have children of our own."

"I'm sorry."

Stephanie shrugged. "My nieces would be better off with me, and Matt has to realize that. No baby-sitter, no housekeeper is going to love them the way their family can."

She wanted to protest, but Matt's sister was right. Emilie Grayson wasn't family and never would be. Her own family consisted of a father who would rather see her in an unhappy marriage than publicly embarrass him. "Matt won't let you take them."

"Of course he will." Stephanie lowered her voice. "He wants what's best for them. Surely now he realizes that hiring a housekeeper couldn't solve everything."

"No," she agreed. "Of course not."

Stephanie hesitated. "Don't be too hard on my brother, Emma. Today is the anniversary of Patty's death. I don't think he ever got over it."

"She died having Mackie?" How could such a thing have happened?

"No. It was a car accident. Mackie was a C-section, right before Patty died."

"I'm sorry," she whispered. "For everyone." She

turned around and headed toward Martha's room. She kissed the girls goodnight, she tucked them into bed, she avoided questions about the television show, and she explained that she might have to leave them for a while and left them to talk with their aunt.

She managed not to cry—not for herself or the children or for Matt. She went downstairs to find Ruth asleep on the couch as the final round of "Jeopardy" ended. She finished cleaning the empty kitchen, removing all traces of the birthday party, and fixed the coffeepot for the morning before she went into her room.

There was no getting around it, she realized. She opened her closet and fingered her wedding dress. It was time to go home. Matt Thomson had hired her to take care of his children. She'd been a make-believe wife, but she hadn't been loved. The woman he'd loved had been killed four years ago. A convenient replacement for a wife, that was all she'd been. He'd never spoken of love and neither had she. She'd cooked and cleaned and taken care of the children. She'd warmed his bed at night.

And she'd never told her boss who she really was—Emilie Grayson, not Emma Gray who she wished she really was, more than anything this moment.

Emilie Grayson hadn't seemed to be very important here on the Triple Creek Ranch. She was a distant memory, a shadow with little substance and even less backbone. Matt wouldn't forgive her for the deception. And he had no reason to.

It was time for Emilie to go home and start a new life. And if she had to start over with a broken heart, then no one ever needed to know. She had loved him, foolish as that was. And now it was time to get over it.

"WHAT DO YOU MEAN, she's gone?" He put his hands on his hips and waited for an answer. He'd spent two hours in his kitchen waiting for Emilie to wake up only to find she wasn't on the ranch at all.

Stephanie and Ruth glanced at each other, then back to Matt. "She left, that's all," his sister said. "She left notes for the girls so they wouldn't be too upset. Wasn't that nice?"

"She left?" He couldn't quite comprehend those words. "How? Where?"

"To North Platte. I took the station wagon and drove her myself. She said she wanted to leave."

"Foolish man," Ruth muttered. "You had a perfectly good woman here and you let her go."

"I didn't let her go," Matt reminded the woman. "Stephanie drove her."

His sister's gaze wavered. "She asked me to."

"And you figured that with her out of the way, you'd get the girls once and for all." He stepped closer to his sister and glared at her. "My daughters are staying here, with me. Is that understood?"

"You said that if you couldn't get help, you'd need me to—"

"I'm their father," he said, softening his voice so Stephanie wouldn't cry. He hated it when she cried. "They need to grow up in their own home."

"I just wanted to help you." She went into his arms and he hugged her to him.

Ruth raised her voice. "For Lord's sake, Steph, leave Matt alone and do something with all that maternal energy and adopt yourself some kids. Heaven knows there's enough out there needing homes."

"That's what Clay says, too," Stephanie sniffed. "I just thought—"

"That you'd have the girls," Matt finished for her. "And maybe you would have, if Emma—Emilie—hadn't taken on the job."

"Bring her back here," Ruth insisted. "She hasn't finished her afghan yet."

"No," Matt said, moving away from both women. He was going to spend the rest of this day outside. He was going to work until he couldn't see straight.

"Stubborn fool," Ruth said, pointing her cane at him. "She was a good girl."

Matt's patience stretched to the breaking point. "She arrived in Lincoln hours before I met her. She came home with me. With a fake name. A fake story. She deceived us, Ruth."

"She took darn good care of us, too," his aunt reminded him. "I didn't see you complaining any."

"No," his sister agreed. "In fact, I think it was exactly the opposite. You were about to kiss her when I walked in yesterday, weren't you?"

He'd done a lot more than kiss Emilie Grayson, but he sure as heck wasn't going to stand here and discuss his sex life with his relatives. Matt grabbed his hat and jammed it on his head. "I'm out of here."

"Foolish man," Ruth muttered. "Letting a good woman get away. Just because of your pride."

That stopped him. He turned around to look at her again. "How did this get to be my fault?"

"You're in love with her."

Stephanie's eyes widened. "He is?"

"Darn right. And he figures she was just playing at loving him back." Ruth shook her head. "You don't know anything about women, Matthew. Just because Patty—"

"Don't bring her into this."

Ruth sighed. "Emma, Emilie, whatever her name is loved you. And you let her go, so it's all your fault."

"Emilie Grayson was about to marry another man. She must have been in love with him. She was still wearing her wedding dress when I met her."

"So that's what's sticking in your craw? Women change their minds, you know." She shook the cane in his direction. "She didn't love that Channing man, whoever he was. She didn't marry him."

"She would have," Matt said, knowing that even right now she could be back in Chicago. He could watch her on television tonight.

Matt figured he'd better go outside and kick his old tractor before he put his fist through the kitchen wall. Love was the last thing in the world he wanted to think about right now. If and when he decided to go after Emilie, it would be his business and nobody else's.

"THE VIEW IS lovely from up here."

"Yes." Emilie didn't glance out the tall windows that overlooked the lake, though Paula seemed impressed with the skyline. She should be; she and Fred lived in an adjacent building.

"He'll come around," her friend assured her. "He's taking you to dinner tonight, isn't he?"

"Yes." Once her father had realized that Emilie wasn't going to listen to his orders anymore, he'd changed tactics. He said he was worried about her. "It's an excellent photo opportunity for the press— Father and Daughter Reunited." Emilie surveyed the empty apartment. She was to sign the lease tomorrow, then she and Paula would begin to decorate.

Today they were to measure windows for the drapes. It would be her first very own home.

If she didn't count the ranch.

"You could go back," her friend said, her voice gentle.

"I can't live at home anymore. Eventually my father would take control again, before I knew it."

"That's not what I meant."

"Oh."

"The ranch, Emmy. The children." Paula looked past Emilie's shoulder and gasped. "The rancher."

"I don't want to talk about—"

"No," Paula said, a smile lighting her face. "The rancher. I think that's him behind you."

Emilie turned to see Matt standing in the doorway. He wore a thick suede jacket and his hair was tousled. He didn't smile. "What are you doing here?"

"Your father gave me this address." He looked toward Paula, stepped into the room and held out his hand. "I'm Matt Thomson. Glad to meet you."

"Paula Lancaster." She shook his hand, then turned to Emilie. "Call me later." Her high heels clicked against the marble floor and she shut the door behind her, leaving them alone in the empty room.

"What are you doing, Matt?" She gripped her hands together so he wouldn't see her shaking.

His gaze never wavered. "I came to ask you to come back home."

"You're offering me a job?"

He shook his head. "I'm offering you a wedding."

"A wedding," she repeated, hoping that she heard him correctly.

"You still have the dress, don't you?"

She didn't answer the question. "If I ever get married, it's going to be to a man who loves me for myself. Not because he needs a wife so he can win an election, not because he needs a mother for his children." There. She'd made the speech she'd practiced so many times, just in case he asked her to come back. Now he could turn around and leave.

"My wife left me. She'd fallen in love with someone else. She didn't even know if the baby she was pregnant with was mine or his. The roads were bad, she was driving too fast, there was an accident." Matt didn't take his gaze from Emilie's face. "I never thought I wanted to get married again, either, but when I do it will be for love and no other reason."

"That's fair enough." But he hadn't said he loved her. She waited to hear the words.

Matt took a deep breath. "I've asked your father's permission," Matt continued. "I know that's old-fashioned, but I thought it was appropriate. He and the girls seemed to be getting along real well."

Emilie didn't even try to understand. "You brought them with you?"

He shrugged. "Stephanie offered to keep them, but I figured they ought to be here for the wedding."

"I'm not marrying you," she insisted, though he'd moved closer and put his hands on her shoulders.

He frowned. "You've patched things up with Channing?"

"No." She couldn't help smiling at the expression on his face. "Ken's not interested in me. He's, well, he's gay."

"Gay."

"He was kissing another man...his best friend... before the wedding. That's why I ran away. I didn't want anyone to know. Ken's a good man and he deserves his privacy."

"And you deserve a husband," the rancher said, his grip tightening. "So come back to Nebraska."

"Do you love me?"

"Would I be here if I didn't?"

Emilie sighed. "Would you please just say the words, just once?"

Matt smiled. And kissed her for a long, satisfying moment. "I love you, Emilie Grayson." He grinned. "How was that? Will you marry me now?"

"Say it again and you have a deal."

"I love you. For better or worse, richer or poorer,

in cowboy boots or ballet shoes." He touched her cheek. "How was that?"

Emilie went willingly into his arms. "Matthew Thomson, you've got yourself a wife."

**Temptation keeps turning up
the heat with**

**Look for these bold, provocative,
ultra-sexy books!**

Available in November:

SCANDALIZED! by Lori Foster

Tony Austin wanted a baby, but he didn't want a wife.
Olivia Anderson wanted a lover, but not a husband. It
should have been the perfect coupling, but sometimes
the best-laid plans don't quite work out. Sometimes
passion can't be controlled....

BLAZE! **Red-hot reads from Temptation!**

Take 4 bestselling love stories FREE

Plus get a FREE surprise gift!

Special Limited-time Offer

Mail to Harlequin Reader Service®

> 3010 Walden Avenue
> P.O. Box 1867
> Buffalo, N.Y. 14240-1867

YES! Please send me 4 free Harlequin Temptation® novels and my free surprise gift. Then send me 4 brand-new novels every month, which I will receive before they appear in bookstores. Bill me at the low price of $2.90 each plus 25¢ delivery and applicable sales tax, if any.* That's the complete price and a savings of over 10% off the cover prices—quite a bargain! I understand that accepting the books and gift places me under no obligation ever to buy any books. I can always return a shipment and cancel at any time. Even if I never buy another book from Harlequin, the 4 free books and the surprise gift are mine to keep forever.

142 BPA A3UP

Name _____ (PLEASE PRINT)

Address _____ Apt. No. _____

City _____ State _____ Zip _____

This offer is limited to one order per household and not valid to present Harlequin Temptation® subscribers. *Terms and prices are subject to change without notice. Sales tax applicable in N.Y.

UTEMP-696

©1990 Harlequin Enterprises Limited

DELTA JUSTICE

**A family dynasty of law and order
is shattered by a mysterious crime
of passion.**

Don't miss the second Delta Justice book
as the mystery unfolds in:

Letters, Lies and Alibis
by Sandy Steen

Rancher Travis Hardin is determined to right a
sixty-year wrong and wreak vengeance on the Delacroix.
But he hadn't intended to fall in love doing it. Was his
desire for Shelby greater than his need to destroy her
family?

Lawyer Shelby Delacroix never does anything halfway.
She is passionate about life, her work...and Travis. Lost
in a romantic haze, Shelby encourages him to join her in
unearthing the Delacroix family secrets. Little does she
suspect that Travis is keeping a few secrets of his own....

**Available in October
wherever Harlequin books are sold.**

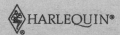

As Seen on TV!

Free Gift Offer

With a Free Gift proof-of-purchase
from any Harlequin® book, you can receive
a beautiful cubic zirconia pendant.

This stunning marquise-shaped stone is a genuine cubic
zirconia—accented by an 18" gold tone necklace.
(Approximate retail value $19.95)

Send for yours today...
compliments of ◆HARLEQUIN®

To receive your free gift, a cubic zirconia pendant, send us one original proof-of-purchase, photocopies not accepted, from the back of any Harlequin Romance®, Harlequin Presents®, Harlequin Temptation®, Harlequin Superromance®, Harlequin Intrigue®, Harlequin American Romance®, or Harlequin Historicals® title available at your favorite retail outlet, together with the Free Gift Certificate, plus a check or money order for $1.65 U.S./$2.15 CAN. (do not send cash) to cover postage and handling, payable to Harlequin Free Gift Offer. We will send you the specified gift. Allow 6 to 8 weeks for delivery. Offer good until December 31, 1997, or while quantities last. Offer valid in the U.S. and Canada only.

Free Gift Certificate

Name: _____

Address: _____

City: _____ State/Province: _____ Zip/Postal Code: _____

Mail this certificate, one proof-of-purchase and a check or money order for postage and handling to: HARLEQUIN FREE GIFT OFFER 1997. In the U.S.: 3010 Walden Avenue, P.O. Box 9071, Buffalo NY 14269-9057. In Canada: P.O. Box 604, Fort Erie, Ontario L2Z 5X3.

FREE GIFT OFFER   084-KEZ

ONE PROOF-OF-PURCHASE
To collect your fabulous FREE GIFT, a cubic zirconia pendant, you must include this original proof-of-purchase for each gift with the properly completed Free Gift Certificate.

084-KEZR